Skoll's Diary

Sean C. Wright

1

Foreword

Dear reader,

I took a big risk with this novel, but a blank page is a blank canvas to do with what you will. I combined two things that interest me: astronomy and rewriting history. 2016 was the start of a hostile political and racial climate in The United States. I got to thinking, what if black folks just up and left Earth, and relocated to another planet in The Milky Way? And how would a black community perform, completely untouched by colonialism?

And truth be told, people of color are quite underrepresented in science fiction. Toni Morrison famously said that if a book doesn't exist that you want to read, write it. That's what I did here.

Skoll, the protagonist, was my medium. He begged me to write his story. I could barely wait to get to my computer for him to pour his story out of my head, through my fingertips and keyboard, and onto paper.

Warning: in this novel, I took a few liberties with the planet Saturn. There's no doubt about it – you will have to suspend disbelief to enjoy this. I made my own wonderland, and rewrote the rules:

1. Saturn is a gas giant in reality. There is only atmosphere. The planet has solid ground in this story, and the same gravity as Earth.
2. I put icy lakes, teeming with seafood, there.
3. Humans adapted to Saturn's atmosphere also, withstanding the intense cold and lack of oxygen in this story.

However, it *does* rain diamonds on Saturn. Atmospheric pressure plays on carbon in its skies, and you get diamond rain. But boo hoo, the beautiful rings are slowly but surely disappearing. Yes, you are reading a novel by a gargantuan nerd.

Not to say something like this story could never, ever happen, but who knows, it still might happen on another planet in The

Milky Way, or one of its moons. There is quiet talk of terraforming Mars one day.

There are other liberties I took, too, but don't want to spoil the story you are about to read.

Thank you so much for supporting my writing. There is nothing more precious to me than the gift of a good story. So hold on to your hats. You're about to take a ride through the stars!

Sincerely,
Sean C. Wright Neeley

*Per herbam ad astra. (From grass to
the stars.)*
-   Latin

Prologue

Nearly all Africans and people of African descent left Earth around the turn of the twentieth century. Although slavery had been abolished, they were still being terrorized, lynched, oppressed with Jim Crow laws, and other indignities. Ignatius (Nat) Blackburn VI traveled to Africa in 1875 to tell the people there of African American suffering in the states. Africans had suffered greatly at the hands of colonization, too. Slavery reduced one-third of the continent's population and the land, too, had been raped of many of its natural resources.

Nat Blackburn didn't just come to trade stories with the African chiefs about injustice at the hands of the white man. He proposed something wonderful, yet outrageous: Let's leave Earth. Why should we stay? The white man will not let us live in peace. And we can do it. Yes, we can. We're the descendants of the original astronomers, scientists, and inventors. Let's decide what planet we want to inhabit, build spaceships, and leave this planet of oppression behind. Project Launch, he called it.

There were chuckles, raised eyebrows at first, but no one dared tell any other ethnic group about it. They'd surely be called a "touched negro," and would lose their housekeeping and train porter jobs. But as soon as Ignatius Blackburn VI started gathering up Blacks with an inclination for engineering to build rockets and astronomers to study planets, people stopped laughing and attended his meetings, little by little.

A Negro cleaning woman, Ola Sparks, who worked for a scientist, nightly sneaked into the lab where they kept a telescope, and taught herself how to use it within a year's time. She subsequently traveled back and forth to Africa with Nat to report her findings. In 1877, the Project Launch crew built and launched one of many satellites to visit planets under the cover of darkness, and analyzed their findings. All the while, they smiled, cooked, sweat, and danced for the white man who had no idea that his help was preparing to leave him high and dry for life among the stars.

Mercury was out of the question because it was too close to the sun. Human flesh – and space suits, too – probably would melt like the wax on Icarus's wings. Venus, "Earth's evil twin" and second planet from the sun, wasn't the least bit hospitable with its constant volcanic eruptions and atmosphere, made of carbon dioxide and sulfuric acid. Mars was a maybe, but it was decided it was also too close. The white man could easily find a way to build spacecraft soon after, and come to Mars. The Milky Way behemoth, Jupiter, has no real surface, as it's a gas giant. Saturn? Maybe. It's strange with its rings and huge, too. Big enough to hold many Earths and has 62 moons. It's freezing, a whopping minus 288 degrees Fahrenheit, but that means plenty of ice. Ice means water. Water. We need a planet with water because then we can terraform it. Uranus and Neptune are too distant. We don't want to get too far away from the sun.

It took 13 tries to find the right material to make a spacesuit that would withstand Saturn's frigid atmosphere. They did it with the help of a teenaged-boy,

Solomon, who worked as a gardener and landscaper by day, but wanted to be a scientist. He lived for the nights that he could contribute to Project Launch.

So many Africans and African Americans became Saturn-bound. Anyone who was not a part of Project Launch was not told which planet they were going to. You had to know the secret handshake to get any information. You see, some decided to stay behind because they were married to people of other races in other countries, where the racial climate was more relaxed. The very old and sick stayed, too. However, some others, married to blacks, decided to go with their spouses. Rockets were furtively built in black people's barns and sheds in America; in some great huts in Africa.

It was all set, Ignatius Blackburn VI, summarized: Africans and African Americans (and a handful of Europeans, Asians, and Hispanics), all over the world would launch their rockets (they fashioned them to launch from inside the shuttle) – full of people, spacesuits, clothes, and food, plant seeds, and soil from Earth - through the roofs of their barns, sheds, and huts, and head for Saturn on March 31, 1900, at a synchronized time in the wee hours. Saturn's orbit put it closest to Earth that day. It would not have been that way for about another thirty-three years. Nat was a young man when he started Project Launch. By the time it was coming to fruition, he was slack-shouldered, heavier, and grayer. But the determination in his eyes was fervent, eternally young.

Whites, especially in the South, noticed something strange about the negroes the day of Project Launch. Maids & nannies seemed happier and more cooperative. Colored janitors sang softly or whistled as they mopped floors and cleaned toilets. Some even gave away household goods: vases, curtains, tablecloths. "I'm remodeling," they explained with good humor. People of European descent who oppressed blacks put the blacks' strange behavior in the backs of their minds that day, and went to sleep with it, only to be awakened by a teeth-rattling WHOOSH, as rockets launched all over the world, carrying away a majority of people who had built America for no pay, fought in wars with little to no recognition, fed and bathed their ivory-skinned children, cooked their food, and danced and sang for them, all while having to use back doors to enter buildings and separate toilets.

They charged out of their houses, and stood outside in their bathrobes and slippers, muttering. Women in curlers. Children holding dolls and teddy bears. Dogs barked. They all looked up with shocked, white faces as hundreds of rockets lit up the sky, and then were gone.

The few blacks all over the world who remained behind, of course, were questioned. "I don't know where they went," they all said in their native tongues. "I just know they went into space."

The two groups built bio domes out of Saturn's rocks. Their bodies changed over the millennia, adapting to their new planet's atmosphere. The dark skin blanched from blue-black or brown to a golden butterscotch because of the distance from the sun. It toughened, too, being able to withstand cold and keep in body warmth for longer periods. Hypothermia would not come to those on Saturn who stayed outside for at least two to three days. The woolly curls became loopy waves, as they no longer needed kinky hair to keep the scalp cool. The eye color dialed back, too, until it became a striking amber. Their lung functions became less and less dependent on oxygen. At first, they needed spacesuits to go outside then they became able to breathe in Saturn's atmospheric buffet - hydrogen, helium, methane, and ammonia - without incident. Their strong features were the only visible traces left of their original ancestry.

The African and African American population, once disconnected on Earth, mixed and morphed into one culture, one tribe: the Saturnaa; the two A's at the end stand for African and American. Swahili, other tribal languages, and Ebonic English interlocked until they became one tongue: Saturnesh. The Africans' Allah and the African Americans' God were the same deity, it was discovered, so the predominant religion was Chrislam (a Christianity and Islam hybrid). They worshipped Godlah, excluding Jesus because slave masters on Earth had forced African Americans to take on the prophet. Both had the common principles of monotheism, not worshipping graven images, and kindness to others. Both groups realized their love of colorful clothing and body adornment. There were tunics of scarlet, gold, cobalt, violet, and striking Earth tones to remind them of home.

Saturn is one of possibly four planets with periodic diamond rain, courtesy of atmospheric pressure, playing on carbon. Saturnaa people catch the clear crystals when they fall from the sky, and wear them in their hair, around their necks, on their earlobes, on their fingers, wrists, and even in their nostrils, even strung together as belts. Decorate their homes with them.

We get a peek into the diary of a bright and sensitive teenaged Saturnaa boy, Skoll, way into the future. He, of course, loves his home planet, but is curious about life beyond Saturn's rings...

March 15, 3005

I am Skoll, named for one of my planet's minor moons. I will be 16 soon. Most of our names are derived from

Saturn's moons, or other heavenly bodies. I was fine with my name until about the age of 9. Someone at learning dome called me *Juth Skoll* (loosely translated, "Numb Skoll)" one day with a sneer, during outside break on the grounds, and I have disliked it ever since. My twin sister, Io, shoved the other boy to the ground, and cracked his tailbone. No one else dared call me that again, but I wished I had a different name after that moment. Titan, maybe. Boys named after that moon are sure to be leaders.

I feel a little rebellious writing down my thoughts. We Saturnaa are a people of oral history for the most part, just like our ancestors on Earth. But I feel like my head will explode if I don't. Io, my sister and best friend, and I share everything. But I just don't feel I can share EVERYTHING with her. Does that make sense?

My father, Mimas, works in the ice mines. They bring in chunks of ice to be melted down to drink, to wash with, cook with, and water the plants in bio domes. Men collect the ice, another group melts it inside the ice-processing bio dome, and another pours water into jugs. Finally, my father delivers jugs to families' bio domes in a heated, rickshaw-like cart. Io and I loved to go on water deliveries with my father when we were little. Every family gets 2 large jugs a day, so Io and I would each take a jug off the cart, once we got up some size, and brought it to the families. It was important that someone be in at the bio dome to receive the jugs. If left outside bio domes too long, the water refreezes. Nothing is more annoying than having to boil your water again, or wait for it to melt when you are thirsty or want to bathe. The people would take full water jugs from us, and exchange them for empty ones, some with a smile. "There's a surprise at the bottom." When we got back to father's cart, we'd dump out the jugs to reveal little cups of *yamolite* (a sweet treat, made of pureed yams and ice crystals), dice made from diamonds to play the game *smeidel,* or small rocks with funny faces etched into them. I still have that rock collection to this day – on display. Sometimes Io comes into my bio dome quarters, smirks, and says, "You still have *that*?"

"Of course I do, sister. Don't you remember how much fun we had in those days? If I have a bad day, all I have to do is come home and look at my rock collection, and I'm happy again."

Io would roll her eyes, take out her learning slate, and settle on the floor. We have studied together since we first started going to the learning dome. I love my twin sister dearly, but she is becoming a real pain these days. She cries at every little thing, spends too time on finding the perfect tunic, and is so fickle about the boys. One week she's in love with Enceladus. Then it's Calypso. "What happened to Enceladus?" dad would ask. Io would twist her mouth, and give another eye roll. Eye-rolling Io. "Enceladus isn't worth his weight in yamolite." He wouldn't ask any more questions after that, but gave our mother, Rhea, a smirk. Our mother has more patience with Io than any of us. "Teenage girls," she explains, "are stranger creatures than the crumbies (crustaceans that live in Saturn's lakes). But she will grow out of it. I promise." I sure hope so. Because some days I want to hug Io, and other days I want to yank her braid as hard as I can, and pull her crazy head right off her shoulders.

Io and I are both good students. My favorite subject is histro-astronomy. It's the study of how we came to be on Saturn and some study of other planets in the heavens. It's not all about facts. We learned about Gleti, the African moon goddess, the star mother. It was believed that eclipses are due to her husband's face occasionally shadowing hers.

I love that class, but wish at the same time that I'd never been introduced to it. Because I wonder about Earth all the time. All the time. Why is it the only other planet in our solar system with life? And diamonds are rare there? How strange and interesting. What's it like to have a twenty four-hour day? Our Saturn days are only about 11 hours. And I've heard the people there are as diverse in color as the flowers there. Most of the little things that crawl on the ground or fly through the air have six legs, except one – an arachnid – that has eight. Eight legs! It's scary and fascinating at once. I've had dreams of blue skies, sunshine, and green grass. Our sky is mainly a filmy shade of purple because we are so far from the sun; and there is no grass.

Our ancestors on Earth had sunshine and grass, but also an oppressive existence, as the logs in the Earth museum show. It's kind of an unspoken and unwritten rule, you are not to think fondly of Earth, or want to visit. That place treated our ancestors terribly for about 400 years. But I can't help it. It really is the planet of our origination, even if it was millennia ago. It can't be a totally crazy thing for me to be drawn to it. Can it? I mean, we were the first humans there.

Anyway, it's time for me to say my prayers to Godlah, and sleep. Goodnight.

March 25, 3005

Happy birthday to Io and me! We're sixteen today. This was one of the best days of my life. Everything seemed sprinkled with magic – until later. Our mother and father had laid presents at the feet of our sleeping mats, so we would see them immediately upon waking. I got 2 new tunics – one gold and the other light green.

Young Saturnesh men wear bright colors to signify maturity. We wear dark tunics when we're young – gray, black, or brown. It's only logical because children spill food on their clothes and get them dirty, playing in muddy ice puddles. A tunic of lighter colors signifies that you are done with all that rowdiness. I can't wait to wear one of mine to learning dome! I also got a ring, shaped like a crumby with diamond eyes, with my initials carved inside it, behind the crumby's head. Io got two new colorful tunics, too, and a matching diamond bracelet.

We went to the eastern Saturnaa market, after breakfast, and walked amongst the vendors, selling tunics, toys, diamond jewelry, bio dome wares, and seeds to grow food in bio domes. Saturnaa families have inside gardens, in back, to grow fruits and vegetables.

Anyway, that's when something strange happened. I wasn't paying much attention at first. My mother and father were looking at a diamond sculpture for the house at a vendor's table, and Io was flirting with the vendor's teenage son. I was standing some distance away from the table with my arms folded, staring at nothing in particular. I was vaguely aware of the other patrons passing then a hunched figure flashed in my peripheral vision. It startled me enough to look in the direction of the movement. It was an old man. His gray hair hung in matted ropes. His silver whiskers were long and shaggy – nearly to his breastbone - and his green tunic was splattered with mud. He was mumbling and gesturing towards the heavens. I don't know why, but I couldn't look away. I didn't realize that the distance between us was closing in, until it was too late. When he was about one foot away, I snapped out of my trance, and turned to go, but he grabbed my shoulders, spun me back around, and pulled me close. The old man smelled of too few baths and bad breath. I noticed he had quite a few teeth missing when he pulled me close. "He's coming! He's coming!" he hissed, his words dripping with an eastern Saturnesh accent, and pointed to the sky.

"Wh-Who?" I stammered, too stunned to pull away. I was hoping he'd say Godlah. Crazy people usually say something like that.

"The man from the blue and green ball," he whispered, and rolled his eyes towards upwards again; eyes that were nearly solid white with cataracts. Then he unhanded me and limped away, mumbling and pointing to the violet sky. He left me standing there, staring after him, my mouth falling down to my chest. I didn't come around until Io shoved me. I jumped. "Wh-what?"

Io rolled her eyes. "I said, come on. Mother and Father are ready to go, and we have been out here two hours already."

"You see that crazy old man?"

Io's eyes scanned the crowds. "What crazy old man?"

I looked everywhere as well, but he was nowhere to be seen. "Well. We better go," I shivered, but I didn't think it was from the cold.

We came back to the bio dome. Io and I had our friends over for yamolite cake, and they gave us presents. It was fun, laughing and talking with our friends, but the old man's words at the market echoed in my brain the entire time. My parents said they would clean up, and sent Io and me off to bed. We had learning dome the next day. Io came into my quarters, without asking permission.

"Are you all right?" my sister asked, her brow wrinkling.

I gave her my best smile, and said, "Of course. I'm just tired. It has been a long day." But Io, being my twin, is an extension of me. I can't fool her. She saw through my lie, like it was air. "No, it's not," she insisted with raised eyebrows. She tossed her long braid over her shoulder. "What's wrong, baby brother?"

I frowned. "You know I hate it when you call me that. You're only a minute older."

"Sorry, Skoll," Io said, looking down. "Really. What *is* wrong?"

I sat up on my mat, laced my fingers together, and looked at my feet. Io came and sat beside me.

"I don't really know, Io" I admitted, "I have…strange thoughts lately."

"Like what," my sister asked gently.

"About the world beyond here. Don't you ever wonder about other planets?"

"Sure," she said.

"Well, I want to experience them; one in particular: Earth. I want to know more than we do in histro-astronomy class," I said in a small voice, regretting it the moment it was out of my mouth.

Io's eyes widened. "You know you can't," she whispered fiercely, "Our ancestors had it bad there. What if nothing has changed?"

I shook my head. "It's crazy, but I feel tied to that planet."

"How? You've never been."

"I know, but our ancestors were there for thousands of years. Its dust is part of my makeup. Part of *our* makeup."

Io puffed up her cheeks, and blew out air. "What made you think of that today?"

"The old man at the market said something to me. I think it was about Earth. There *was* an old man."

Io wrinkled her nose. "I'm not saying there wasn't. I just didn't see him. Anyway, don't pay attention to what some crazy old man said. His brain is probably full of crumbies."

"You're probably right," I said, sighing. "Well, we better get to bed. Happy birthday, sister," I said softly, looking at her.

"Happy birthday, brother," she said with a soft smile. She hugged me before she got up off my mat and left my quarters.

I wrote this entry with a shaking hand before going to sleep.

March 31, 3005

Today is Saturnaa Independence Day, the 1105th anniversary of the day we left Earth. There was a diamond festival in the square and a city ceremony. Whenever we have a diamond storm, road workers collect the bigger pieces that fall from the sky. The purpose is not only a safety issue, but for artisans to make jewelry and other decorations out of them.

I love this time of year. There are so many proud Saturnaa people in colorful tunics and diamonds on every limb, music, dancers, food, and art vendors. My family attended, and I met my best friend, Atlas, by the statue of Nat Blackburn VI, as soon as I got there. We went off by ourselves, and watched the dancers for a while. There were twenty men and eleven women (that equals thirty-one; the day we left Earth), dancing, all in clear tunics. The clear tunics signify diamonds, and they have white bands, wrapped around their privates for modesty. Their kicks, twirls, and shakes were in perfect synchrony to the drums and *gara* (a type of horn) and *unime* (a stringed instrument) that the musicians played nearby. It's likened to what our people on Earth called "jazz," originating there in 1895.

My stomach knotted. I stole glances around, expecting the old man to approach me, like he did at the market.

"Are you all right, Skoll?" Atlas asked.

"Why?"

"You just look like you've seen a ghost, or you're expecting to see one."

"Yes. I am fine. There's just a lot to see here. So many amazing sights," I answered, raising my eyebrows and smiling.

The dancers had wrapped up with a final lunge and kick.

I clapped Atlas on the back. "Let's go get a yamolite cup. My treat," I said.

He grinned and we started off towards the food vendors. Nobody approached me at the festival, but I still stole a look around here and there. I could barely concentrate on Queen Andromeda's speech, which was towards the end of the festival.

Queen Andromeda looked quite beautiful, younger than her 68 years. Her silver waves were braided about her head and coiled in four big knots, secured by diamond pins as big as babies' fists. Her silver tunic shone like evening stars. In closing, Queen Andromeda instructed us to bow our heads, and close our eyes in prayer. I lowered my head, but didn't dare close my eyes; I only lowered them, shifted them side-to-side. Oh, I *did* pray. But I didn't pray to Godlah for what everyone else prayed for: more Saturnaa prosperity. I prayed that I wasn't losing my mind.

April 30, 3005

Sorry I haven't shared my thoughts in a month.
I have been busy.
I am in love!

Her name is Dione, named after one of Saturn's bigger moons. Atlas says they named her that because her "chest moons" are so large. That is the first time we ever argued. He apologized, said he was only teasing. I hope it's the last.

Anyway, Dione sits next to me in Saturnesh class. She gets high marks like I do, and creates/recites some of the most beautiful Saturnesh poetry. She is a tall, full-breasted girl (Atlas is right, but it was still disrespectful) with a full mouth and gentle, amber eyes, flecked with brown. She weaves a strand of diamonds through her waist-length braid (Saturnesh girls do not wear their hair any other way until they marry), and only wears scarlet tunics, which must be her favorite color.

I asked her to go to my favorite place, the histro-astronomy museum, with me one weekend. My heart did 3 flips in a row when she said yes. There was another diamond storm earlier that day, and I prayed to Godlah that it would stop by the time we made our plans. My prayers worked.

We had a really good time, looking at models of the solar system and at the historic wing. It has space suits, parts of the aircraft that brought our ancestors to this planet, and replicas of sacred journals, encased in glass, that tell our history on Earth and early history on Saturn. I took a while, studying this part of the museum, as I always do. I nearly forgot that I had someone with me. I looked around, embarrassed, but only to find that Dione was doing the same thing. She was planted in front of one of the open journals, her face nearly up to the glass. She was mouthing the words. I stepped towards her. Dione turned her face to me, her eyes sparkling, like the diamonds in her hair, and said, "Mac-aroni."

"What?" I asked.

"Macaroni…and cheese. That was one of the African American dishes on Earth," she said in a low voice, still staring at the worn, open book behind the glass, "That's what it says."

I went towards the glass, and scanned the loopy writing. Sure enough, there it was. I had heard of cheese, but never tasted it. It was made from the milk glands of Earth creatures, which we didn't bring with us when we left Earth. We felt milk was only

30

for babies. But what the nebula was macaroni? Great Godlah, it sounded like a skin rash. That thought was out of my mouth before I could stop it. Dione turned from the display, and bust out laughing. I joined her.

We walked arm-in-arm through the streets after we left the museum, our destination, a café that served some of the best crumby stew. We sat down on floor mats and the waiter came to take our orders. "I'll have the macaroni," Dione said. The waiter frowned. Dione and I laughed again. That day pushed the encounter with the old man in the market to the back of my mind.

May 5, 3005

Good Godlah! Something happened two nights ago. Something fantastic and scary at the same time. So I cannot keep my journal under my sleeping mat, like I did. I now keep it strapped to my side, under my tunic at all times. I can't risk anyone finding it. So, here goes…

I couldn't sleep that night. I tossed on my mat, like a crumby caught in a net, then flipped on my back, and just stared up at the rock ceiling in my quarters. Sleep still didn't come. I got up, and grabbed my sitting mat, and took it outside to the back of our bio dome. I figured fresh air would calm me. I sat comfortably, on the ground, underneath a pitch-black sky that was dotted with many glowing moons – big and small - and Saturn's multicolored rings, arcing over my head. It was peaceful. I smiled at some of my thoughts: Dione and her bubbly personality and sweet eyes. Atlas, being silly at lunch break at the learning dome. Some of the private jokes that Io and I share.

Then, it happened.

I saw something floating in the heavens in the corner of my eye. I nearly broke my neck, turning my head to look at it. It was gliding, and coming closer and closer to us, it seemed. The middle was cylindrical, and bore two wide panels, like outstretched arms. I watched with huge eyes and a hanging jaw.

I don't know why, but I followed it, only to look around to see if anyone was awake, seeing this too. But, no. The rest of Saturnaa was fast asleep. I kept walking until I hit Saturnaa's northern border; entranced. I hadn't even realized it until I saw our village's flags on poles - red, black, and green cloths with a rhombus-shaped diamond superimposed on the front - flapping in the lunar wind.

I stood at our border, and stared at the curious thing in the sky until it went down. How far away was it? A mile, maybe a little less? I stood there forever, trying to figure out what to do. A sixteen-year-old boy should not leave our city's confines without an adult escort. The minimum age to do so is twenty. I should have run home, gathered up my sitting mat, and gotten my butt back to my quarters. But I didn't. It was as if this curious thing pulled me along by a string; tethered. I walked in the direction of the billowing smoke. I still stayed about ten feet away from it. Since the sky glider was cracked and smoking, I figured it was damaged. This was not a live thing, but a machine. It looked familiar, too. Where had I seen something like it? Ah! In my histro-astronomy books. Our ancestors sent these out to explore other planets. They are called sat...*satellites*. We knew they were some sent to Saturn, since we settled here, but never this close to Saturnaa. Our planet is so big, that we have been lucky for millennia not to encounter them, but have a drill in place, just in case: we're to tell Queen Andromeda immediately if we encounter any evidence of intelligent life on our planet.

I stood there, looking down at the broken machine with my hands at my throat. And the old man's words at the market echoed in my head; made a frigid wind blow inside me. I had to tell my father who would take me to the queen. But wouldn't I get in trouble for leaving Saturnaa with no escort? Of course. I had broken a law. I looked around again, and up at the sky, which would lighten in a few hours. I looked down at the machine again. It stopped smoking. The smoke cleared enough for me to make out an image on the side. I'm doing my best to recreate it from memory:

I have seen that flag before. The satellite was from a country on Earth! I don't know why I did what I did next: I dug a shallow grave for the machine, and put its debris inside of the hole. I then covered it up with a few rocks, ice and diamond chunks. Even though no one was around, I kept looking over my shoulder.

I jogged home, washed up, and went right to sleep. I only got to rest for about two hours. It seemed as if I blinked, and it was time to rise, and get ready for learning dome. I went through the motions during my lectures, taking notes. My mind was not there. It was in the ground with the satellite, outside of Saturnaa's city walls.

May 10, 3005

I am trying to keep my secret, but it has been difficult. I am coming apart. Sleep doesn't come easily, my marks are falling, and Dione has commented on how distracted I have been. Things have been so bad that I did something three nights ago that I wouldn't have dreamed of doing before all this happened: I sneaked into the kitchen and poured myself a cup of my father's *yamake* (a drink, made of fermented yam paste and water). It did help me sleep. I only planned to do it one night, but there I was again, the next night, pouring another cup when everyone else in my bio dome was asleep. I replaced what I took with water.

I can't keep living like this. And I can't keep drinking myself to sleep. I have to tell someone what I found.

Godlah, please give me the courage to do this. And please forgive me for keeping this secret.

May 12, 3005

I plan to tell someone about what I found about two weeks ago. The question is who? 16 is such a confusing age. I still want my mother and father's guidance, but want my independence. Mother Rhea is sweet and patient. She would never judge me. She's at the top of my list. The problem is, she will tell father immediately. Io is my other half, and wouldn't really judge me either, but she isn't very level-headed, she would go running to mother and father immediately. Father Mimas has always been a fair man, but I know he will be very disappointed in me. I haven't known Dione long enough to tell her. I need more time to think. That's it. I need more time. But this is something that can't wait for too long.

May 15, 3005

I've made my decision: I will tell
mother and father both today, without Io
present. I will instruct them not to tell her
right away. My twin can always sense when
something is going on with me, but when
she asks, I'll simply tell her it's "private boy
business." Io will probably wrinkle her nose,
and stop asking questions.

May 17, 3005

I did it. I waited until after dinner, last
night. I finished my studies immediately, so
that would be out of the way. The hardest
part is over. It wasn't as bad as I thought it
would be. I guess you know because I'm
writing this that father didn't murder me,
and throw me into Lake Calypso.
Anyway, I waited until Io went to her
quarters. I went up to mother and father's
quarters, and quietly asked through the
privacy curtain if I could come in. They told
me to wait. I guess one – or both of them –
were getting decent (gross). Mother Rhea
pulled back the curtain and pulled me in to

the room by my wrist. She and father sat on their sleeping mat. After what seemed like forever, I closed my eyes, and confessed. "I couldn't sleep the other night, and went outside to sit under the stars. I saw something in the sky and followed it…" Yes, I left Saturnaa's borders without an escort. Yes, I realized it was something that could put the Saturnaa people in danger. Yes, I concealed it for over two weeks. And please don't tell Io right now.

I opened my eyes, only to find tears leaking from them. I'm not going to lie. It was embarrassing. I am a young man now, and I was weeping like a boy. I caught sight of my father's face through my haze of tears. He was scowling, and trying to keep his composure. Then his face softened. My mother gasped then jumped up from their sleeping mat to hug me. Sweet Mother Rhea! She knows that a little boy is still wrapped up in this young man. She rocked me in her hug, and cooed to me that she was disappointed at first, but proud of me for telling. Her voice was as sweet as the Saturnesh lullabies she sang to me and Io when we were small. Her effect tamped my father's anger, too. He stepped forward, and hugged us both.

I broke the hug first. I took a step back, but still kept my head down. My father spoke in a low and slow tone. "First thing tomorrow, we will go see Queen Andromeda. You will tell her what you told us. But don't tell her how long ago this happened. As far as she needs to know, this happened tonight. They will probably want you to take them to where you hid the satellite. Your mother will tell Io and your classmates that you are ill. Now go to sleep, and try not to worry."

I left my parents quarters obediently, and did what my father asked. It was the first night in a few days that I went right to sleep without needing a cup of yamake to do so.

May 18, 3005

Today is the day. We go to see Queen Andromeda in a couple hours. Since I am not going to learning dome, I have time this morning to make an entry in my journal. I put on one of the new tunics I got for my birthday. My heart is going in my chest, like nimble hands on drums. For all they know, I simply didn't tell anyone about this at first because I left Saturnaa with no escort. They don't know about my preoccupation with Earth, and don't need to know…

I have to go. Mother is calling me to come have breakfast. I must close my journal and strap it to me, under my tunic. More later.

May 31, 3005

Forgive me for the long pause in entries again. Much has happened since we visited Queen Andromeda with my news. Father and I were escorted with 4 of Saturnaa's soldiers, to the site of the buried machine. The ride in one of the castle's carts out there was stern. It seemed more like 10 miles, instead of about one. When we finally got there, all I could do was stand there with down-cast eyes at the slightly bulging ground that kept my now-revealed secret. Father Mimas gently nudged me forward, and said in a low voice, "Go on, son. Start uncovering it." I obeyed with shaking hands, the rocks and diamonds I used to cover the machine in the ground felt much heavier that time.

When I got it uncovered enough for pieces to show through, the quartet of soldiers began to grunt and frown. The stocky one with a heavy beard held up his hand, and said, "We'll take it from here." I stepped back, and the soldier's crowded around the broken satellite. They spoke in quiet, secretive tones. Heavy Beard must have been the leader because he turned to father and me, and said, "We will need your help to load it into the cart," in a flat tone. We loaded the pieces into the cart, silently. With 6 of us working, it went fast.

Once finished, Heavy Beard spoke again, "There will not be enough room for everyone to ride back in the cart. You have two choices: we can go back and send another cart for you, or you may walk back to Saturnaa." I knew immediately what I wanted to do. Being with those men was like having someone's hands, squeezing my throat.

"I'd rather walk back," I said, "if it's fine with father." Father Mimas looked spent from the manual labor, but also relieved. I don't think he liked being in the soldiers' company any longer than we had to be either. The soldiers grunted again, and rolled away in the cart with the satellite, hidden under many cloths.

Anyway, my father and I said little on the walk home. I could tell he was still disappointed in me. I had narrowly escaped punishment from the government. I had left the grounds without a chaperone, but did bring something very important to the government's attention. I was advised to get an adult to escort me, or send him or her in my place next time. This was my first and last warning on this situation. Next time, I would be sentenced to do work on the days there was no learning dome – emptying and hauling refuse from the bins in the city square. That's the punishment for Saturnaa teenagers. Adults who break our laws, depending on the severity of the offense, get fined, or spend time in the castle's dungeon. No one is mistreated in the dungeon, I've heard. You get decent food, may wear your own clothing, and are taken out for fresh air for two hours a day – once at day, once at night. You even get counseled. They try to get to the root of why you committed the offense. I must say that Queen Andromeda is a very fair ruler.

I went back to learning dome the next day, feeling like my old self again. I could pay attention in class, and joke with my friends. I apologized to Dione for my mood, explaining that there had been a family emergency, and I wasn't dealing with it well. That wasn't a lie. She twisted her mouth, then offered me a soft smile. There was peace in my life again. Thank Godlah.

June 5, 3005

There was an assembly yesterday. The messengers came through the streets, blowing hollow crumby shells to alert everyone to meet in the square. If they blow once, it's just a message. Two short blasts mean an emergency. Good thing it was only one blast this time.

We gathered in the square with expectant expressions. One of the queen's guards helped her up the steps to the natural rock pedestal. She looked as lovely yesterday as she did during the festival in a silver tunic with ruffles at the neck. This time, her hair was braided in 2 plaits, and pinned across her head, like a halo. She wore her diamond pins stuck in the braids so closely together that they looked as one; a crown.

While Queen Andromeda was getting settled, Dione and I caught each others' eyes. She gave me a sly smile then turned her eyes back to the queen.

"Hello, everyone," Queen Andromeda began, "thank you for coming on short notice. I'm afraid I have good news and bad news." The crowd groaned, and the queen cleared her throat. "The bad news first; a satellite crashed near here, about a week ago, in the dead of night. It's from Earth." The crowd gasped, and Queen Andromeda held up her hand. "Please, everyone. It's going to be all right. Here's the good news: the satellite malfunctioned and crashed before it could get any clear images of our settlement. Our technicians were able confirm that when they did tests on it. The images it sent back to Earth just made Saturnaa look like blobs of rocks and ice chunks. We are still keeping up the illusion that Saturn is void of life. And please, notify government officials immediately if you see anything else foreign or strange."

There was some gasping and head-shaking amongst Saturnaa residents. Queen Andromeda stiffened her spine and swallowed. "Please be assured that myself and the government are doing everything to keep the Saturnaa people safe. There is no cause to worry. We're handling this. Thank you. That is all. Now let us pray." We all bowed our heads.

After the crowd broke up. Dione came up behind me and grabbed my hand. She tugged me behind a secluded bio dome. She didn't have to say a word. We kissed.

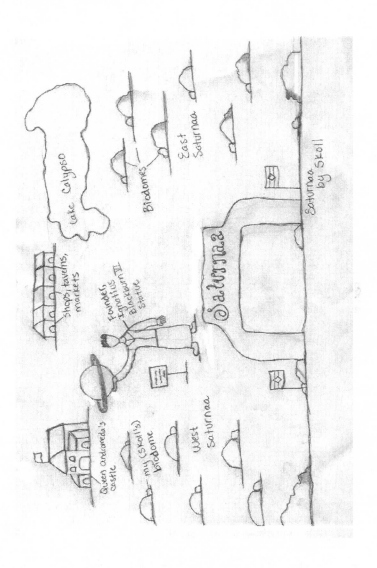

47

June 10, 3005

Since we're so far away from the sun,
we Saturnaa people catch its rays with solar
panels, filter out harmful radiation, and turn
it into liquid. The golden fluid, solar juice, is
then mixed with water to nourish plants in
our bio domes. We also drink it to nourish
our bodies, keep our vitamin D levels
healthy. Solar juice is expensive, so you
won't find a solar juice bar on every corner
in the Saturnaa streets. But this day, I was
craving some. I wanted to celebrate things
getting back to normal. I asked Atlas to
come with me to the solar juice tavern – my
treat. His eyes lit up, but he smirked.
"What's the occasion?" he asked.

"There is none," I said with a shrug,
turning my crumby ring around and around
on my finger, "I could just go for some solar
juice."

That was enough to convince Atlas. He
started whistling as we left his bio dome and
started into the roads towards the juice bar.
It was going to cost nearly half my

allowance – 5 *nats*. Our currency is named after our founder. The coins are round, polished crumby shells with relief carvings of Ignatius Blackburn VI's image on them.

The tavern is warm inside because of the solar juice warmers. It must be kept warm to keep its nutritious properties for both the plants and us. Atlas and I sat on a mat with a little stone-carved table between us in the middle of the place. A waiter brought us a bowl of peanuts, and asked for our order. I just wanted plain solar juice. Atlas asked for it with small yam cubes. I like the drink plain to get the full benefit of the flavor. It's hard to describe exactly what it tastes like. It's sweet-tart with a crisp finish.

I felt carefree as Atlas and I were talking and joking and sipping our liquid sun drinks. I was with my best friend in a warm place with a good drink. What could be better?

Anyway, I excused myself to go to the toilets, around back. I was full of liquid sun and fun, distracted. As soon as I put my hand on the knob, someone grabbed my wrist. I jumped back to find the old man from the markets about three months ago. "Wha-What do you want? Why can't you leave me alone?" I nearly shouted.

"Because you know. You *know*," he hissed, pointing up to the sky, and looking up at it with cataract-filmed eyes.

"I don't know what you're talking about. Now leave before I have the owners to toss you off this property," I scowled.

The old man stared at me for a few seconds longer, not saying anything. His expression nearly looked sad for me. Then he turned and hobbled away, mumbling in that raspy, eastern Saturnesh accent of his.

I barely made it to the toilet in time.

June 13, 3005

I didn't tell Io about the old man bothering me again at the solar juice house. Damn him to the bottom of the Lake Calypso! I thought I was done with his madness, and the big mess with the satellite. How does he know where I will be, and keep showing up there? That crazy old man makes me afraid to go anywhere, but to learning dome. I will complain about him next time if he bothers me. They will surely grab him by the collar and seat of his smelly and tattered green tunic; heave him into the icy mud. I hate to be cruel, but he best leave me alone.

Anyway, I have a project to do for learning dome, due in about three days. It's a diagram of The Milky Way. I must say that my art skills are exceptional, and I always get high marks on diagrams. I better get to work.

June 15, 3005

I gazed at my project (We make paper from vegetable pulp, and ink colors from vegetable dye), realizing that I paid much more attention to Earth than I did to the other planets. I wrote the most detail about its planetary habits, life, etc. It was as if a ghost took hold of my hand, as I worked with the stylus. But I was tired, and I would have to start over to fix the error. There wasn't time, as it was due the next day. It might raise the professor's eyebrows, but he couldn't fail me on the project, as I did the minimum of what was asked. I shook my head, as I rolled the project into a scroll and tied it with a string, yawning. I said my prayers to Godlah and went fast asleep.

We'll see what mark I get on the diagram soon.

June 21, 3005

I was worried for nothing. Professor Comet did only state that he wished I had given the other planets equal coverage on my diagram, but gave me a good mark anyway. I think my detailed artwork saved me. I must admit my hands trembled when I filled in Earth's globe with swirls of deep-blue and green.

Anyway, what else is new? Io is becoming even more of a pain these days. She refuses to eat crumby now. It's Cruel, Io says. It's Murder, Io says. She says she will get protein from ground nuts from now on. She even went so far as to keep a live crumby in a water-filled pot in her room as a pet. We'll see how long it lasts. Io sits at the dinner table, eating her vegetables and nuts with an occasional longing glance at our plates when Mother Rhea cooks and serves crumby. I have fun with it sometimes. "Mmmm-mmm, this fried crumby is soooo delicious," I declare. Io scowls and I smirk. My parents give me a glare, but all I do is chuckle.

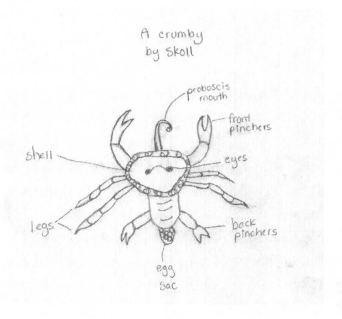

A crumby by Skoll

proboscis mouth

front pinchers

shell

eyes

legs

back pinchers

egg sac

June 25, 3005

There was a meeting tonight. Men gathered under a canopy in the marketplace and discussed concerns. Similar meetings were being held in north, south, and east

Saturnaa as well. Recorders take notes on scrolls to the castle for Queen Andromeda and her advisors to review. This is the first year that I could attend, having just turned sixteen.

Father Mimas and I sat together on the mats we brought from our bio dome. To be honest, I found most of the talk boring. The Western Saturnaa representative droned on about taxes, regulating yamake, redrawing quadrants (eastern Saturnaa complains that there are not enough buildings in their part of the settlement), etc. I looked off into the distance, got distracted by a shooting star until I heard the representative say something about the satellite from Earth. Father kept a stoic face, while I squirmed, turned my crumby ring around and around on my finger. Thank Godlah that no one seemed to notice. A thin man with sleepy eyes in a tan tunic clicked his tongue and raised his eyebrows before he spoke. "Queen Andromeda said there was no need to worry, so we shouldn't. Let's not waste our time on that." I released a trapped breath as the other men grunted in agreement.

Father and I stole sneaky glances at each other. He put a hand on my shoulder.

On the walk home, Father Mimas proposed that we go to a tavern for some yamake. I was so surprised that I stopped walking. "Just one, son. You're getting to be a man. But don't tell your mother," he said with a chuckle. I let father think that was the first time I tasted yamake. However, it didn't make the moment between me and my father any less special.

July 1, 3005

No learning dome today. There was a severe diamond storm last night. Thank Godlah that not many homes or buildings were badly damaged, but some of the roads were clogged with rocks, as big as toddlers, that the crews needed to clear.

It's just as well. I am ill today. Io was sweet. She brought me warm crumby broth and a little yamolite to soothe my scratchy throat. I dozed on my sleeping mat with the comfort food, churning in my stomach, and Mother Rhea singing a Saturnesh lullaby.

I don't know how long I had been asleep before the bad dream started. It didn't start out as a bad dream though. I shrunk down, small enough to walk on my solar system diagram. I leapt right off the two-dimensional sketch of Saturn, and jumped onto Earth without a second thought. Then the pulpy paper, beneath my feet turned into real grass. Grass, that I had only read about. I could see the blades clearly, sticking up here and there. Flowers preened in the grass and warm breeze in bright, happy colors. I had only heard of colored jewels, unlike clear diamonds, and I felt like I was in the middle of a colored jewel. I looked up and the sky was blue, not light purple. It was so beautiful with swirls of wispy white going through it and a glowing, yellow sun. I stood there, wide-eyed, mouth agape.

This is where it got scary.

All of a sudden, I was in total darkness, crowded with other people, and in chains. They were moaning and crying and praying. Then I was strapped to a post. I man with pink skin and beady, blue eyes held a whip. He shouted at me in a language I couldn't understand so closely to me that I could feel his hot breath on my nose, yet I understood that he was going to punish me. He went behind me, and whipped me. I screamed. Then the scene of the horrible dream involved Father Mimas. He was suspended on a tree limb by a long, thick string, his feet desperately kicking the air. He was choking and his eyes were rolling back in his head. Pink-skinned men were holding everyone back with weapons, smiling cruelly. I was in the crowd with the rest of my family, and we were weeping and begging. Other people were there too, trying to comfort us. "Father!" I called. "Father!"

Father Mimas shook me awake. "I'm here, son. I'm here!" I was sweaty, wild-eyed. Without another word, I hugged my father. "Oh, father," I said, "I had a terrible dream where you…got hurt." He rubbed my back, and replied in a low voice, "No one is going to hurt me. You were just fever dreaming. Now lie back down. I'll have Io bring you more crumby broth and water."

I obeyed. He was barely out of my quarters before I yanked my blanket over my head, and wept.

I felt such relief when Mother Rhea checked on me before she went to bed. She said I didn't have to go to learning dome tomorrow. Being sick and the bad dream has made me weak. It was a real effort to make this journal entry. With that said, goodnight.

July 5, 3005

I had dinner at Dione's house tonight. Her mother is not as good a cook as Mother Rhea, but it was passable. Anyway, we went for a stroll in the back of Dione's dome, in the garden. A bio dome's garden is a wonderful place to relax and talk. It's warm back there because of the solar juice. The warm air and the green ground must look like, well…Earth. I found myself staring at the yams, onions, and cucumbers, pushing up from the ground.

We build so many things as humans, and take such boastful pride in it. But Godlah's works are most amazing with their simplicity. Nothing but soil, seeds, and sunlight yield food.

I turned my gaze from the ground, and focused it on my Dione. Dione's sparkling, yellow eyes and easy smile make everything better.

July 10, 3005

Good news! I applied to SLOT (Saturnesh Leaders of Tomorrow) and got accepted. The minimum age is 16, and many Saturnesh get their start in government with this program. I leave learning dome about 15 minutes early each day, and meet with an advisor who has a city task for me. One day, I helped workers clear diamonds from the roads after a storm. Another day, I took small children to the histro-astronomy museum. Father Mimas was not in SLOT, but his father was. You don't get paid any *nats*, but you earn awards. Plus, it's good experience.

This is my cure for my preoccupation with Earth, I'm sure. My pride in my people and planet grows with each task I complete.

July 13, 3005

Io is SO ridiculous. She is back to eating crumby. She let her pet crumby go in Lake Calypso last weekend. I think we just should have fried it up. Ha! I so wanted to tease her, but couldn't. I don't know. Maybe I'm growing up.

July 21, 3005

Good news again. A select few of us (10) in SLOT will go to Queen Andromeda's castle to get a tour of the government department, and see if we want to do some tasks there. It will happen in two weeks. Mother Rhea and Father Mimas expressed their pride in me. Io even kissed my forehead. Then father took us all out for solar juice. Another wonderful day. I am going to have yamolite-sweet dreams on my sleeping mat tonight. I welcome them. Between learning dome and SLOT, I am tired, but it's a happy tired. Does that make sense?

Goodnight and Godlah bless.

July 27, 3005

Atlas and Dione surprised me with a congratulatory present at lunch today: A chain of peanut-sized diamonds. It goes nicely with my diamond-eyed crumby ring. I have such a great best friend and girl.

August 10, 3005 AM

Today is the day we go to Queen Andromeda's castle. I had a quick moment to make this entry before breakfast. I will write about the whole experience tonight.

August 10, 3005 PM

What a wonderful place the inside of the castle is! I tried my best to keep my composure, and not look like a young boy, seeing a diamond storm for the first time. (Father Mimas and I delivered a message to the castle about the satellite. We were not allowed in then.)
We entered the first floor. It looked like a big bio dome's living room. There

was a large mat for sitting with a large, round stone-carved table in the center - where the advisors sit with the queen. The table's centerpiece is a bowl of diamond chunks, as big as oranges. The walls are adorned with artwork from the past and present: Ignatius Blackburn VI, a scene at Lake Calypso, Saturnaa at sunrise, a picture of our original planet, Earth (my eyes snagged on the image longer than it should have), and portraits of our other rulers. There is a small canteen in the corner with limitless yamolite and solar juice. There are many windows; I counted 6. Most Saturnaa homes only have about 2 in the living area. Glass is expensive because it's difficult to deliver. Heating the dirt, and making it into sheets is not really a problem here. However, carrying that fragile cargo to buildings on the bumpy roads of rocks and ice is.

A fireplace warms the advisor room, like a mother's bosom. It was attractive, but not unnecessarily extravagant. Our leaders never misuse tax money for their luxuries.

The tour guide was one of the queen's guards and assistants. He's a tall, man with stern, hazel eyes. He must have a handful of European blood. He wore the required ivory tunics of the government official with diamond-button plackets. "Hello, and welcome to Saturnesh castle," he stated, in clipped and formal Saturnesh, "My name is Neptune. We are very happy to have you here, you bright young men…" Neptune went on to show us around the advisor's room. I got chills, being in the same room where laws and major decisions are made.

The adjoining room was the Bureau of Logs. Saturnesh political history and noteworthy happenings are recorded in volumes and stored here. The scribes looked up from their writing mats at the ten of us, and gave us a little wave. No one smiled. I guessed it was because they were trying to concentrate on the facts.

After that, we got a tour of the dungeon, underground. Thanks goodness it was empty. "I hope none of you ever have to stay down here," Neptune said, drily. It looked like a bare-bones place, but not a cruel place. The rumors were true: you are treated humanely in the dungeon. We don't have that much crime anyway. There's little reason to steal, as we Saturnesh share everything. There has never been a war – not even a civil one - and only a handful of murders in all the millennia that we've existed.

Neptune showed us the kitchen and cafeteria, where you could get a steaming plate of boiled crumby and vegetables for a nat.

After the tour, Neptune had us all wait in the cafeteria. He then called us into the advisor room one-by-one, asking what tasks we'd like to do at the castle. I asked him to put me down for a scribe intern, as I have a penchant for writing. Neptune looked pleased. After our mini interviews, we were all given souvenirs – diamond paperweights with the Saturnesh flag etched on them – and dismissed.

Now, I wait. We will see if I get the scribe intern. My family, Atlas, and Dione are all keeping their fingers crossed for me.

It has been a long day. I can barely keep my eyes open. Goodnight. May Godlah be with you.

August 17, 3005

I am a scribe. I am a scribe. I am a scribe. Yes! They start training me next week. Father took me shopping for a new vest to wear for this honorary duty at Andromeda's castle.

I am excited for me, but worried about my sister, Io. She has been acting strangely. Her skin is waxy and she always looks on the verge of tears. I asked her what's wrong, but she won't tell me now. "I'll tell you later," she said. I asked if anyone hurt her, or threatened to hurt her. She shook her head. Mother and father can't get anything out of her either. Io pretty much told them the same thing: "I'll tell you soon." I hope my sister isn't dying. It will be like half my heart dies too if my twin sister goes to Godlah now. We are growing apart, but the bond is still forever. I will say a prayer to Godlah for my dear sister, Io, before going to sleep.

August 20, 3005

I wore my new vest today to the castle for my first day as a scribe intern. I left learning dome fifteen minutes early, like I usually do for my tasks. I was strolling down the road to the castle, absentmindedly, humming and kicking rocks and diamond pebbles when suddenly I felt as if I was being watched. I stopped and whipped my head around: the old man. He stood by a large boulder in that ragged, green tunic of his, like a statue, gazing at me with those filmy, white eyes. As I said before, I was tired of his foolishness. I wasn't afraid. Well, maybe a little. The road was deserted. But I wasn't going to let him know that. "What do you want?" I hissed through clenched teeth. The old man said nothing this time, just stared. He gave me a sad look, mixed with a frown, then slowly turned and limped away. I shook my head, and continued on my way. I wasn't about to let that old fool ruin my day. But I was somber the rest of the walk.

I am apprenticed to a scribe, named Pluto, a little man. His ivory tunic hangs on his small frame like a blanket. Pluto doesn't look like he has much going on in that little body, but he is a wizard with a stylus and grammatically correct Saturnesh. For my first day, he had me reading a few volumes of some of the first logs ever written on this planet. They are written in English with Saturnesh footnotes as translations. Since English is one of the languages that Saturnesh is based on, you can actually understand some of the English. I memorized some of the English words, and said them aloud on my trudge home. They are not as fluid as Saturnesh. English sounds harsh, but noble: *space, rocket, stars, eat, drink, smile, cry, laugh.*

I didn't see the old man in a green tunic again that day. Thank Godlah. I went home, and told my parents about my first day, which they were eager to hear about. Io stayed in her quarters. I got the feeling I was not to disturb her.

August 22, 3005

I am picking things up as a scribe fairly quickly. Pluto is pleased. I have read all the logs he assigned to me for fundamentals, and I started recording things today on paper. I was to take all the notes from the meetings from every district, and combine them into one log. I made few mistakes, but Pluto said they are natural for beginners. He is confident that I am on my way to being a fine scribe. Pluto told me that was all I was assigned today, and I was free to go, but I asked him if I could stay a little longer, and study past logs. He raised his eyebrows and grinned. "That is fine with me," Pluto said, "I wish all of our interns were so into history and government as you." His only advice was that I finish my cup of solar juice before reading the logs. Food and drink are forbidden near them. I finished my drink, grabbed a couple of logs, and settled myself on a mat against the wall. By the time I left the castle today, I was fluent in one line of English from the logs: "Hello. My name is Nat Blackburn VI. My people left Earth March 31, 1900..."

I ran the line by Dione, and her eyes lit up and she smiled, as if I did an amazing magic trick. Like I pulled a diamond from thin air.

August 30, 3005

We know what's wrong with Io. But I cannot bring myself to write it down just now. Father Mimas called a family meeting last night. Io sat at the table, her eyes swollen and red. She kept them down most of the time, and nervously fingered the end of her long braid. Mother Rhea dropped her head in her hands. My mouth fell open at the news.

Our family goes to the priest, St. Jove, before morning Godlah service tomorrow. We will have him make arrangements. My parents will have to go to learning dome on Monday, and tell them that Io will be out ill for a few months.

I can't believe this, my twin sister, Io, had such a bright future. I was angry, but sad for her. I made her stand up after the meeting, so I could hug her. She began to sob and hug me back, like she never wanted to let go. I can't even tell Dione about this…

September 4, 3005

I am still in shock over Io's news. But who am I to judge? I'm nearly a man, dreaming of a far-off place, beyond the stars. Io made a mistake. She didn't do it alone, but she still feels so guilty that she disappointed herself and our family. I can do nothing, but love her for now. Io stays in her quarters now, most of the time, reading books that I bring her, and asking about her friends. We told everyone that her illness is contagious, so there are to be no visitors. I have persuaded her to come into my quarters a few times to keep me company while I study after I return from Andromeda's castle. I joke with her and try to stay upbeat. It's the first time I have seen my sister smile in months.

September 7, 3005

I have been throwing myself into my scribe task at the castle to take my mind off things at home. When there is nothing to record, Pluto allows me to read about our government and history. I have taken quite an interest in Saturnesh law. As I said before, crime is low here because we are such a close-knit community, but there are exceptions to every society. Thus, rules must be in place. Thieves must apologize to their victims, return the stolen property, and spend one week in the dungeon to get counseling. Young people who offend must do work for the city as punishment (Like I might have been made to do when I left the city's walls, unescorted), and must get counseled with St. Jove for however long Queen Andromeda sees fit.

Felons aren't treated with such rationality though. Rapists are given one of two choices: if you want to remain among us, you must be castrated, and of course, get counseling. If you do not, we will send you to one of Saturn's moons. Murderers are not castrated, but are sent to another moon, as well, if they choose not to get counseling. We don't believe in the death penalty. It's up to Godlah when someone leaves this life, not humans. There has never been one rape on record, and only 2 murders in our whole history. One was in 2072. The other was in 2080. Both offenders got counseling, and found Godlah again. They lived their remaining days without incident.

There is also a policy on what to do if Saturnaa was ever discovered by other intelligent life, but it is sealed. My eyes have caressed that volume every time I go near the old scrolls, but I don't even dare touch it.

I am picking up more and more English, enough to introduce myself and ask a person's name: "I am Skoll. Who are you?" To say "food" when I am hungry, and "water" when I am thirsty.

October 7, 3005

Sorry it has been a month since I wrote. Much has happened. Father Mimas' work days have been cut back from 5 to 3. The water delivery company has two broken carts, so workers can't deliver water until they are fixed. One has a broken axle and the other's heating mechanism is damaged. It's only temporary, but fewer deliveries mean fewer nats for father.

Pluto has become like a big brother to me at the castle. He gave me a stylus, and sometimes buys me a plate in the castle cafeteria. Sometimes, Pluto sends me home with solar juice for Io once I mentioned that she had been sick. It really does light up her face.

October 15, 3005

My heart is broken.
She wasn't mean about it.
She was even tearful when she told
me.
She didn't mean for it to happen.
I offered to return the diamond chain
necklace she gave me, but she insisted I
keep it.
Dione broke up with me.
Dione fell in love with Titan.
I can't believe this. That *megop* (a
timid person; void of personality)! There is
nothing remarkable about Titan. Titan
doesn't hurt anyone, but he doesn't help
anyone either. I am a good writer and artist,
and am doing things for the Saturnesh
community. What does Titan have to offer
Dione? The boy jumps at his own shadow.
Io has been especially sweet after
hearing the news. She comes into my
quarters after I get home from my scribe
business at the castle. The roles are reversed
for now. She tries her best to lift my spirits.
The twin bond we share is always and
forever.

October 21, 3005

Godlah answered my prayers. The carts are fixed at the water delivery company, so Father Mimas is back to work, 5 days a week.

I am nearly over Dione. Io and Atlas have been wonderful. I do better some days than others. On especially bad days, I imagine Dione in Titan's arms, and feel sick. It's hard to be with Dione every day in Saturnesh class, but I try to look over her head, not right at her. And it's not easy to ignore her statuesque, red-clad figure, but I manage. I nearly snatched my rope of diamonds from my neck that Dione had given me, and tossed them into Lake Calypso on my way to the castle. Then I remembered that it was a gift from Atlas, too…

I have been focusing on my tasks at the castle more and more. I am getting better and better at English. I hope to be fluent – or close to it - by year's end.

November 3, 3005

Io's time came as soon as the sun pulled up.

I ran to Atlas' house, and told him to tell our instructors that I would be out today, and that I wouldn't be doing my scribe duty either, as we had a family emergency. Atlas looked at me strangely. He then promised to relay the messages.

The midwife, Helene, named after a medium-sized moon, is 96-years-old, but is as sharp and capable as a 30-year-old. All I could do was gawk, as Mother Rhea led Helene to Io's quarters where her screams funneled out her quarters, and echoed throughout our bio dome.

Helene, the midwife, is a solitary woman. She never attends assemblies, and it's rumored that she relies on her neighbors to relay any important information that Queen Andromeda divulges. The old midwife is tall; I would say an even 6 feet. Strong; she carries no cane. She wore a soft-blue tunic today and harnessed her waves in immaculate Bantu knots with tiny diamond pins, sticking out of the tips. Her regality nearly rivals Queen Andromeda's.

Anyway, the sun was directly above Saturn's rings by the time my nephew screamed his way into the world. We all went in to see him and Io, as soon as Helene said we could. Io was on her sleeping mat, smiling weakly through her tears and sweat, as she held her son. "Janus," she said hoarsely, "His name is Janus." Janus is a small Saturn moon, but means the "beginning and end."

And how beautiful Janus is! He has golden skin and downy, reddish hair. And I could have sworn that he smiled, at just a few minutes old.

Io is to have one week with the baby. She is to have another week, recovering, before she returns to learning dome. Then the childless couple that St. Jove arranged to take Janus will come and collect him. They are to keep Janus until Io finishes learning dome or moves out of our home – whichever comes first. Then Io may have him back. Father Mimas will deliver Io's milk to Janus, during his water deliveries, until he eats solid food. We are allowed to visit with the baby.

Io has never revealed the baby's father. She refuses to.

November 18, 3005

It's a sad day. The couple comes to get Janus. We may visit him, but it's not the same. My beautiful nephew brightened our home with his sweet baby smell and sleepy, toothless smiles. And all that will be gone this evening. We all took turns comforting my weeping sister, as soon as they left with her son.

December 1, 3005

I hit my goal before deadline. I am fluent in English before year's end. My accent is probably not correct though. But how would I know what is the "correct" English accent? I have never heard English spoken. It's still better than nothing. I am one of the elite. Only the scribes in Andromeda's castle know English, but they are not fluent. There are words I know now that I want to experience: *sunshine, grass,*

rain (with water drops, not diamonds),
birds…

Sometimes…

Sometimes, I feel Saturn's rings are
prison bars. Why am I the only one? We
Saturnaa know there's intelligent life on
other planets, but we're not allowed to
communicate with it. Don't others here find
that frustrating, too? This is where I really
envy Earthlings. They live in ignorant bliss,
thinking the other Milky Way planets are
void of life. They don't know about us, but
we know about them. But then I remember
how horrible my ancestors were treated on
that lush, marbled globe, once upon a time,
and it makes my jaw clench. I pray to
Godlah that this is a phase I am going
through. Please, Godlah, let it be that. I
don't want to do something again as foolish
as that business with the satellite.

December 15, 3005

The last two weeks have been a blur. I keep my head down in my studies, focus on my scribe intern. Dione and Titan are no longer together. I don't care. I really don't. I have more serious things to worry about with Io and all. Dione hasn't attempted to get back with me, but I can tell she realizes that she was impulsive about leaving me. At least we talk a little again. I think she knows I forgive her. But truth be told, I don't think I can be with anyone right now.

Between the satellite discovery, the old man sightings, and Io's problem, it has been quite a year. I am so glad that 3005 ends in two weeks. I will pray to Godlah to bring me and my family an easier time in 3006 before I lay my weary bones down on my sleeping mat.

December 31, 3005

We send off the old year with a huge festival, Year-End Fest. It's only one of two city festivities, the other one being the anniversary celebration of when we left Earth that I mentioned before, in March. Year-End Fest is my favorite of the two. It's a time for unity, praise; peace amongst the Saturnaa people. I heard the Earthlings often said Peace on Earth during their holidays. That's the same concept here for Year-End Fest: goodwill towards men, love, and thanking Godlah for our blessings.

There's so much love and fun in the air. Every family brings food to share with the community, so there's an endless buffet laid out on mats: crumby dishes, seasoned vegetables, fruits, breads. Children, 12 and over, are even allowed a sip or 2 of yamake for this special occasion. The musicians played feverishly, and people danced, laughed, fellowshipped. It was a sea of smiles, colorful tunics and sparkling diamonds on fingers, necks, in hair, and on wrists. People picked up children who weren't theirs, kissed them and danced with them.

Janus's surrogate parents brought him to Year-End Fest. Io held Janus for a while, kissed his plump cheeks. I SO wanted to join her. As far as anyone could tell, she was just doing what everyone else was doing at the festival, and loving on the children. I could tell she was trying very hard not to cry. She did very well, and handed her baby back to its "parents" with downcast eyes. I noticed Atlas's head and eyes dropped at the whole scene. Then he suddenly nudged both Io and me, nearly having to shout over the music, saying, "Come on. Let's go get another serving of yamolite before it's all gone." I shrugged and followed. Io lingered a moment, staring at the woman who held my nearly two-month-old nephew who gurgled and drooled on her shoulder, and then joined us. That was the only low point in the party.

I was very full of rich Saturnaa dishes and a little tipsy from the yamake when we all looked at the sky to see the sun, slowly peeking up over the rings. When it made its full debut, the music stopped, and we all bowed our heads at Queen Andromeda's instruction. We prayed for a fruitful new year. It's kind of somber, the passing of the old year and all. I read that Earthlings welcome the new year with celebratory fervor. We Saturnesh give the old one a "funeral."

Anyway, hello, 3006! I am tired, but there is no learning dome tomorrow; no scribe internship. I get to sleep in.

January 28, 3006

A new year calls for new goals. Father Mimas resolves to cut back on yamake; Mother Rhea resolves to make fried crumby less often. "It's bad for the heart," she says.

My new year's goal? I somehow get the feeling that it's important to translate this journal into English. I don't know why. I mean, who's going to see it? Hopefully, no one. But it will be a fun project.

Something is wrong with Atlas. I have asked my best friend what is the matter, but he just looks at the ground and shakes his head, mutters, "nothing." Other times, he seems like he wants to tell me something, but stops himself. He looks sad. He looks guilty. "Is it about a girl?" I asked Atlas at lunch one day when we were alone. He looked off into the distance, and mumbled, "sort of." I told him whoever broke his heart was not worthy of him. And I reminded him how he told me the same when Dione broke up with me. He just sighed and shrugged. I figured it wasn't my right to keep prying, so I stopped. He does ask how Io is doing on occasion though, which is very nice of him.

Everything else is going well though. I haven't seen that pesky old man anymore.

February 29, 3006

Queen Andromeda died.
She was 69.
I am so sad.
We are so sad.
She was one of the best rulers the Saturnaa people ever had, and she was the only queen I have ever known. Queen Andromeda reigned for 50 years, all of them good. The minute she came to the throne, at 19, she promised to care for her people, as if they were her family. And never once did the queen go back on that promise. She attended every funeral, and sent birthday wishes on paper to every child until they reached 18. I still have my 16 copies of birthday wishes from the castle on papyrus,

personally signed by Queen Andromeda.
Sometimes, men in the castle tried to
intimidate her, but she was firm on her
policies. She was a kind woman with a
diamond-hard spine. Sure, people who
worked for the government live better than
those who do not, but those favors were cut
back anytime people in the village were not
getting basics. Tunics on every back;
crumbies in every pot, was her motto. She
was a godly queen, too, working with St.
Jove at the temple to accomplish her
mission. It was said that Queen Andromeda
often dropped by there to ensure there was
enough clothing and food for people to
come by and get it, should they need it.

She will be sorely missed.

She will make a beautiful angel.

Queen Andromeda's funeral was
beautiful. The musicians played tunes no
softer than a whisper. Her corpse was laid
on the royalty platform, a jutting and
naturally occurring plank of ice where all
deceased kings and queens before her were
laid. She was swaddled in ivory cloths,
fastened around her with diamond chains.

Torches were lit around the platform. Everyone in the village lined up to say goodbyes, and give small gifts for her to enjoy in her journey to Godlah's house. Queen Andromeda was then buried in a secret location with her gifts. Only the people in the castle know where.

Artists paint our leaders' portraits every year in case they pass away, so the most recent one may be hung in the castle. I saw Queen Andromeda's portrait in the castle when I reported there for scribe duty 2 weeks after her death. It's lovely. The artist captured the fierce determination in her eyes with her soft smile.

Queen Andromeda's brother, Pulsar, is in line to take the throne next. He is 65. (Andromeda never had children to succeed the throne, due to numerous miscarriages and one daughter who only lived for a few days. Her husband proceeded her in death, 5 years ago.) Even though they are cut from the same cloth, Pulsar surely has a tough act to follow.

Rest in peace, Queen Andromeda. January 15, 2937 – February 7, 3006.

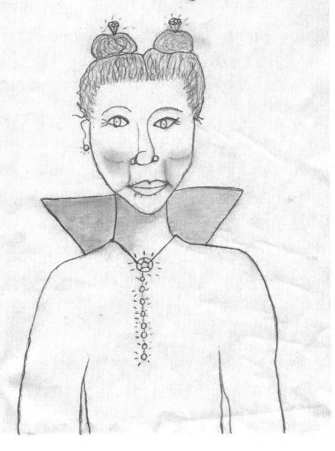

Queen Andromeda
by Skoll

March 5, 3006

It's Saturday. We visited with Janus's surrogate parents today. They are nice people. They know how hard this is for Io and my family, and almost always say yes when Father Mimas asks if we may visit when he delivers Io's milk. We never stay more than an hour. We don't want to take advantage. I fight the urge to smuggle my nephew out of their bio dome in my tunic. He belongs with us. But it's Saturnaa law that teenagers cannot parent their children because they are not mature enough. Grandparents aren't to raise their grandchildren along with children they already have in the house because it's considered too much of a burden. It makes sense to the head, but not to the heart.

Io always goes to her quarters after these visits. She refuses to even come out for dinner. I sometimes hear my dear twin sister sobbing.

March 17, 3006

It has been nearly a year since I started this journal. I will have to start a new book, as this one is getting too bulky to strap to my side. I better think about another hiding place for this one – and fast. I alternate between adding to this and translating what I already have written into English.

Mine and Io's birthday is coming up again. What a difference a year makes. I feel like I have grown 10 years, instead of only one…

I still don't know what is wrong with Atlas. I am a little angry that he won't tell me. I am his best friend. He knows I won't tell anyone, and that I will do nothing, but support him. It must be pretty bad. I have a good relationship with his parents, and considered asking them what is wrong, but stop myself. I just pray to Godlah for him.

March 25, 3006

Io and I are 17! This year, we opted to go the histro-astronomy museum and out for lunch afterwards. Of course, there was yamolite and fellowshipping back at our bio dome.

Atlas didn't come. One of my other friends gave word that he was sick, and would not be attending the festivities. I have a feeling that Atlas wasn't being truthful…

Anyway, Io and I got more beautiful tunics and a bottle of yamake each.

I didn't see the old man anywhere today. Maybe he is finally leaving me alone. But why did he bother me in the first place?

April 8, 3006

Janus is now 5 months. There are 2 tiny, white buds on his bottom gums. He gurgles and smiles more and more. Io sings to him when we visit. We leave my sister alone with her son for about 30 minutes then our whole family visits with him for the other 30. Janus is a bright one; I can tell. He has an intelligent gleam in his eye, and is very curious. The precious babe nearly pulled my diamond necklace off when I held him. I did nothing but chuckle while I uncurled his tiny, chubby fist from the jewels.

April 16, 3006

A poem that was crawling around in my head, like a crazed crumby:

Saturn's looping bands are colored like my thoughts
Violet, when I feel passion
Orange, when I feel joy
Blue, when I feel sad
Off-white, when I feel nothing in particular
Green, when I think of another place, light years away, closer to the sun
Shags of soft green on its ground, like a chunky-knit tunic
It dances closer around the sun
Warmed like a child, held in his mother's bosom

April 25, 3006

My hands are shaking, as I write this. I know what's wrong with Atlas. I am FURIOUS! I can't say what's going on just right now.

May 10, 3006

My beautiful nephew, Janus, is about 6 months old now. His features are becoming distinct. I saw something familiar in that little face, especially in the eyes. Images began poking at my memory, like a crumby's spindly, venomous tongue: Atlas's detached behavior since Janus was born. His mask of shame and drooping shoulders, every time he was anywhere near Io…

I asked permission to enter Io's room 2 nights ago, after dinner. Upon her consent, I entered with clenched teeth, pulled the privacy sheet across the threshold, looked her right in the eye without so much as a breath before I fiercely whispered, "Atlas is Janus's father, isn't he?"

Io's mouth dropped and she looked at me, eyes round and shiny as new nats. She had been sitting cross-legged on her sleeping mat, working on what I assumed was a learning dome assignment, and dropped the stylus in her hand. Her silence answered my question. We stared at each other for a full

10 seconds; me in quiet fury, Io in cold shock.

Io rose from her mat, rushed towards me, and grabbed my shoulders. "Please," she begged in the same fierce whisper, so mother and father wouldn't hear, "don't tell." Io began to cry.

"H-how could you not tell us? What happened? When did you date?" I had so many questions in my head that it spun.

My twin sister let go of my shoulders, looked down and to her right. (I'm doing my best to paraphrase what she said.) "W-we didn't. When I spent the night with my friend, Mercuria, last year, she pushed me to meet her boyfriend and Atlas at Nebular Point (a cave where young people to hang out, get drunk on yamake, and write dirty Saturnesh words and pictures on the cave's walls), after her parents went to sleep. I-I really didn't want to, but didn't want to kill the mood. We all got drunk. Mecuria and her boyfriend went deeper into the cave, leaving Atlas and me alone. I had always liked Atlas. He admitted that he always liked me, too. You can guess the rest…"

I stood staring, my chin nearly hanging on my chest. I closed my mouth, and turned my ring around and around on my finger.

"What did Atlas do when you told him you were pregnant?" I asked softly.

Io began to cry softly again. "He asked me if I was sure it was his. He is the only boy I have ever been with, Skoll."

I sighed. "Io," I moaned. "Sneaking out to meet boys, getting drunk…we were raised better than this. What are you doing?"

My twin sniffled, and looked at me with wet eyes.

"I-I wanted people to like me. All these years as a good student, and everyone giggling about what sdren (Saturnesh for nerd) we are. It got to me. I'm not like you, Skoll. You don't care what anyone thinks of you. You are a good artist and a good scribe, dear brother. I have nothing, once we leave learning dome. Nothing, except Janus."

And then, as if Io read my mind, she whispered, "Please don't do anything to Atlas."

May 15, 3006

My best friend fathered my nephew.
My nephew has my best friend as his
father.
Atlas is Janus's father.
No matter which way I write it, it
sounds terrible. I have spent the last five
days with one foot in a secretive place,
keeping this from my parents and Atlas',
and another foot in a hot, furious place with
the rage I feel towards Atlas. How could he
not tell me?

May 22, 3006

I confronted Atlas. I asked to speak to
him alone, during mealtime at learning
dome. We walked away from everyone,
towards the toilets. Atlas, with slumped
shoulders and downcast eyes; me with
clenched fists.
"I know," I said in a low voice,
looking right at him after we stopped
walking, facing each other.

Atlas jerked his eyes up, and tried to smile. "Know what, *rafiki* (friend)?"

"You must think I'm stupid!" I whispered fiercely.

Atlas tore his eyes away, and muttered, "I don't know what you're talking about."

"You have five seconds to admit it, or I will pound your head, flatter than a crumby shell!" I was nearly shouting by then.

"Io told you?" his voice crackled.

"It doesn't matter *how* I found out. And, no, Io didn't tell me until I confronted her."

Atlas swallowed then looked at the sky. His tone was so low that I barely heard him. "We never meant for it to happen. We were both drunk."

"I get that, but why didn't you tell *me*, your best friend, that you got my sister pregnant?"

"I-I." Atlas began to cry before he could finish the sentence. I noticed someone coming from the corner of my eye. Without hesitation, I grabbed my best friend by the wrist, opened the boys' toilet door, slung him in, and closed the door. I stood in front of the door with both my arms stretched wide, barring entry. "It will be just a minute. Someone is sick in there." The other boy shrugged, and walked away.

And just like that, my anger dissolved. I suddenly remembered why Atlas was my best friend…

Atlas had told no one that *I* had cried because I had tumbled off a huge ice boulder we were playing on when we were 8.

Atlas had me laughing like crazy when he put a woman's tunic on Ignatius Blackburn's statue in the square when we were 13.

Atlas brings containers of nuts and raw vegetables to school, and shares them with students who have no lunches. Been doing that since we were 12.

Atlas, dear Atlas, who recently got me through that terrible break-up with Dione.

Yes, Atlas had made a mistake – a huge one – but a mistake. Godlah makes no one perfect. Godlah forgives. I knocked softly on the door, telling him that no one was around, and was he okay?

He stepped out, gingerly, and nodded. He wore a mask of fear. "Let's get back to lunch before they miss us." He nodded again, seemed to release a trapped breath, and we walked back to the learning dome building in silence. I put my palm on his back as we walked.

May 25, 3006

The next day, I told Atlas and Io that I wouldn't tell our parents or his. It's their secret to tell anyway.

May 27, 3006

I saw the old man yesterday, again while I walked to the castle. He stared at me, pointed towards the heavens, and said, "In 4 days."
I said nothing.
I scowled.
I snorted.
And I kept walking.

June 7, 3006

Oh, Godlah. It is amazing! We are not to leave our bio domes until further notice. I can't believe this. More later.

June 11, 3006

So here goes. As soon as the sun pierced night, (it was May 31; exactly 4 days after I saw the old man, and he said "4 days") the horn sounded twice. We all looked at each other. An emergency! What could it be? The square was a flurry of multicolored tunics and twinkling diamonds on limbs, as we all hurried outside in an orderly fashion (we were instructed never to run because someone could get trampled).

I could see its huge, pointy tip, standing 3 times taller than the statue of Ignatius.

A rocket has landed here. From Earth!

June 12, 3006

King Pulsar instructed everyone to remain calm. It's hard to get use to seeing him, instead of his sister, Andromeda. He seems to like the celebrity of his role more than the actual role. His manner is as ostentatious as his clothes: diamonds on every finger, both earlobes, and a diamond pendant around his neck the size of an orange.

There were guards, surrounding the rocket. The man from Earth has been taken into the castle's custody.

I pushed through the crowd to get a better look at the rocket. I couldn't see the whole thing because a guard stood in the way, but I saw enough. I stood there, with my mouth hanging open, staring, my head swimming with memories. I realized, with a chill climbing my spine, that they had been warnings. The old man in his dirty, green tunic and his cryptic messages. That flag, that flag, that flag with its stars and stripes…

The rocket had the same flag on it as the satellite! Evidently, it doesn't take 6 years to get here from Earth anymore, the way it did in the 20th century. It merely takes months.

I didn't hear King Pulsar dismiss us. Someone had to nudge me to get me moving.

June 19, 3006 am

On June 8, nearly a week after the Earthling landed in Saturnaa, there was a knock at our bio dome door, and I answered. It was Pluto. He told me that I am needed at the castle to speak with the Earthling. They think he speaks English.

I can't describe what I felt.

Excitement, but fear.

Grown-up, but young and vulnerable.

I wanted to hide behind Mother Rhea's tunic folds, as I did as a child. But I couldn't do that. I am now a man.

My mouth went dry while my palms and underarms churned rivers. My voice sounded so small and crackly. "I have to ask my parents."

Pluto frowned. "It's not a request," he said gently. "You are the only one on the planet who speaks English fluently. I know enough to get by, but we need someone who knows it well. The whole Saturnaa fate is at stake. Come." Pluto nearly sounded like he was begging when he said the word.

"All right," I said, my heart hammering in my chest, "at least let me tell my family where I will be."

Pluto nodded.

I invited Pluto in, and called out to my family. They had all been dozing on and off since we had been prisoners in our homes. They came to the front of the house with drowsy eyes that widened when they saw Pluto. He greeted them, explained the situation. My parents and Io tried not to look worried, but didn't succeed. Pluto noticed. "Do not worry, Lord Mimas and Lady Rhea. We will take good care of him. It may only be for a few hours, tops. I will walk him back, as well."

My family hugged me tightly, though, as if I were going on a long trip. I asked Pluto if I could change before we left. He said yes. I went to my room, and hurriedly dressed in one of my best tunics to meet the man from Earth.

June 19, 3006 pm

I wish I could say that I was confident in meeting the man from Earth for the first time, and that English flowed off my tongue, like a cascade of solar juice.

But it didn't.

Oh, so many sights and sounds to take in! They put him in the castle's dungeon. He still wore his space suit (a puffy, white thing that looks pretty comical) – to protect him from our intense cold - but has been fitted with an oxygen mask they got from the histro-astronomy museum. It still works. We got the oxygen from farmers, who sell it to us, along with solar juice to nurture our plants.

I stared through the bars at him, my tongue as dead as crumby in my mouth, left out of water too long. He looked SO strange, and frankly, not particularly attractive. His skin was a color I had never seen, kind of like a combination of very light red & ivory. I think the English word is "pink." We have no tunics of this skin color. His hair was long and peculiar, like individual threads all over his head, and yellowish. Yellow hair! His eyes were blue. We Saturnaa are mostly amber or light brown-eyed. A few have green eyes; some hazel, but never blue. Blue? I take that back. Here, only blind people have that eye color. I vaguely wondered if he was blind.

But no, the man from Earth could not fly here, blind. For he was peering at me through the bars with the same curiosity, those blue eyes nearly bulging over his mask. I must look a sight to the Earthling, too. A peanut-skinned teenaged boy in a golden tunic with a snug rope of diamonds at the neck. Curls, falling this way and that, stopping at the nape of his neck.

I got so caught up in all of it, that Pluto had to nudge me between my shoulder blades to break the spell. I jumped and blinked. "Names should come first," I thought, turning my crumby ring around on my finger, two, three times.

A hoarse voice came from someone. I was in such shock that I didn't realize it was me at first. I wanted very much to say, "What is your name?" but the words wouldn't roll from my head to my mouth. "Skoll," I said, pointing to my chest. I pointed at him, through the bars. "You? Name?"

The Earthling relaxed, ran a hand through that strange, cropped yellow hair of his, and replied, "Jeffrey. Jeffrey McNeely. Jeff." He nearly smiled. I think it was because he was so happy to have someone to communication with on this planet, and also because he realized that I hadn't come to hurt him.

"Jiff?" I stuttered.

"No. *Jeff*. Call me Jeff."

"Jeff."

"Yes...Skoll."

"I am hungry. I have food on my rocket. Can you tell them to bring me some?" he asked, gesturing to Pluto and the guard outside the cell.

I understood every word, but all I could do was nod. Pulling Pluto close to me, I whispered the Earthling's request in Saturnesh. Pluto gave a curt nod, and left me alone with the Earthling and the guard.

"Food coming," I said. What was wrong with me? That was *not* good English.

"Thank you, Skoll," he muttered.

I stood there, staring. The Earthling dropped those blue eyes to the dungeon floor, and a flush came to his cheeks.

June 29, 3006

NASA, a space program on Earth, sent Astronaut Jeff McNeely to explore Saturn. He and NASA (from a country called America on Earth. That's an American flag I saw on his rocket.) They thought Saturn was void of life, as the satellite showed them, last year.

Fortunately for us, Jeff landed here after the sun had fallen. All of Saturnaa was asleep, and the homes looked like huge rock masses when he sent recorded pictures of our planet back to Earth. He was discovered shortly before daybreak and taken into custody, while still asleep in his rocket, before he could send back any more recordings.

Every morning, Jeff is escorted back to his rocket to talk to his recording machine that feeds back to NASA. Someone remains off camera, holding up words in big print for him to read (I write the letters because I am the only one fluent in English.) I can tell he is afraid, even though I told him that no one here means to hurt him (at least I don't think so yet.) Jeff has been instructed to tell NASA that his camera on his spacesuit helmet broken, so there will be no recording while he explores. In truth, the guards destroyed it. The illusion is still in place that Saturn is life-barren. As far as they know, Jeff McNeely is the only person who has ever been here. This plan was written in the logs, centuries ago, in case someone – or something – comes to Saturnaa.

I have been summoned to the castle every day for the past 10 days. I pick Jeff's brain, and translate it to Pluto who then makes notes to give back to the king. I miss the normalcy of going to learning dome, but this is a piece of a dream come true. I didn't go to Earth. A piece of it came to me!

We still don't know what to do with Jeff. As with any prisoner here, he isn't mistreated, but he is still a human in captivity. It's sad. He committed no crime.

July 4, 3006

My visits with Jeff are always supervised, but the guards do not understand what we're saying. His food supply from the rocket is dwindling. He's supposed to return to Earth in a week. I persuaded them to let me bring him a bowl of crumby soup and a cup of solar juice.

Jeff frowned when he saw me with the food and drink, and the guards unlocked the door for me to bring it to him. I set it on the small pedestal in the dungeon before him that acts as a tray. I explained what I brought him, and why. Something like a smile came to his lips. I had a slight longing to see his face, completely free of the oxygen mask.

"Do you mind if I talk to you while you eat, Jeff?"

"Not at all," he said, still eyeing me.

I smiled at him, and pointed an open palm towards the food and drink. That snapped him out of his trance, and he picked up the spoon. I muttered over my shoulder to the guards that I would be talking to Jeff as he ate, and that it was all right to close the cell door.

I had so many questions that I hardly knew where to begin. What do birds sound like? What is it like to walk on sand? To swim in warm, salty water that goes with the sand? What do flower petals feel like?

For some reason, all I could squeak out was, "How's the crumby stew?"

"It's actually delicious. It tastes like, I don't know, like a cross between sea animals we eat on Earth. They are called crabs and lobsters. This meat feels like crab meat on the tongue, but tastes a bit sweet, like lobster. The vegetables in here taste very fresh. Mmmm-mmm." Jeff gulped and chewed.

"We grow them with solar juice and oxygen. You have a cup of solar juice right there. Drink some before it gets cold. It's best warm," I said. He took a sip, and his eyebrows rose in pleasure.

"Jeff? What are black and brown people up to on Earth now?" I immediately wished I hadn't asked that. Why didn't I ask about birds or beaches?

He stopped eating, and put down the spoon, his strange, blue eyes, pensive above his oxygen mask, as he studied me.

"They are few in numbers, as so many of you came here so long ago. There are no more full-blood Africans. They are all mixed with other races. It's actually very attractive."

I digested the information, imagining brown people on very green grass, under very blue skies.

"And Africa? What of Africa?" I squeaked.

"What do you know about that continent?"

I got the feeling Jeff was being evasive.

I shrugged. "Only what I have read in the logs here. That it is very warm with beautiful plains and animals. Giraffes, lions, rhinos. I have only seen sketches, only heard descriptions of their colors."

"It's pretty much gone," Jeff mumbled.

I raised an eyebrow. "What do you mean?"

"Other races inhabited it, used up everything, then left. There are no more natural resources from there – diamonds, cocoa beans. We haven't seen real chocolate in centuries. They make imitation chocolate from carob. These diamonds that you and the other Saturnaa wear are so amazing! I never thought I would see so many real diamonds in my lifetime. The only ones we see are in museums."

I was suddenly angry.

"And the animals?" I said in a low tone.

Jeff dropped his head. "They went extinct about 200 years ago."

"It wasn't enough that you made my ancestors slaves, and mistreated them after that, but you completely destroyed their land, too?!" I was nearly shouting.

Jeff snapped his head up, and shook and shook it. His blue eyes wide. "I had nothing to do with that. This all happened hundreds of years before I was born. It was a terrible thing, slavery and everything after.

"I know all about your ancestors leaving because of the mistreatment on Earth. My wife, Zinnia, is one-fourth black, and has schooled me thoroughly on black history. She ensures that our daughter knows her black ancestry as well. She is ten months. Her name is Aurora. Please let me see her again."

Jeff stopped speaking, and choked. I thought it was the crumby soup, but he hadn't been eating. Suddenly, his blue eyes were leaking.

I felt badly for him, and hated him at once. He had a family he felt he might never see again, but now he knew how our ancestors felt, being held hostage by people who looked differently than him; not knowing his fate. My ancestors had cried those same terrified tears in the bellies of slave ships, and behind bars for crimes they didn't commit. I wanted to comfort him, and then slap him.

Instead, I said, "Drink your solar juice before it gets cold," and turned to leave.

Jeff reached out, and grabbed the sleeve of my tunic. "Wait, Skoll! Don't leave! What are they going to do to me? I didn't come here to hurt anyone, and haven't."

"That's because you *can't. We* have all the power. How does it feel? It's not up to me anyway," I nearly spit.

Jeff said nothing to that. He let me go, hung his head, and slowly reached for his solar juice. I called for the guards.

There is to be a meeting in two days to decide what to do about Jeff. I am the only student who is allowed to attend because I have been talking to him. No pressure there.

July 5, 3006

The day before the meeting, I went to the castle, but didn't visit Jeff. We had all the information we needed to present in the meeting.

I looked at the logs again, specifically the notes and sketches on Africa. I could tell even in those two-dimensional sketches that it had been a paradise. Its sun, glowing orange through wide, twisted trees. Beige, majestic lions with fierce eyes. Zebras dressed in swirling black and white, grazing on green fields.

Gone.

All gone.

I twisted my mouth and closed the book on Africa, absentmindedly looking for something else to read. There was a heavy and bulging log of crime cases. I grabbed it, opening it to a random page...

Case # 369, the year 2502 AD

Cassini, a wiry man of about 30, was captured in the square, mumbling to himself.

On occasion, he would say something coherent. Something about going to Earth to assassinate an Earthling. "It's the only way to save Saturnaa! Who's with me?" Cassini cried. Nobody really paid attention to him until he started piling up rocks to build his "spaceship," and "recruiting" people to help – giving them rumpled pieces of papyrus that he deemed flyers on the mission.

Cassini accosted people in the square, and frightened young children with his ranting and raving, and ragged appearance; his green tunic was filthy, and his beard grew to his sternum. His hair had not been washed or combed in weeks.

Cassini could no longer be ignored, so Saturnaa authorities picked him up, and questioned him. He kept pointing up, and insisting that an Earthling was coming. The Earthling was not born yet, but Cassini had been ordained by Godlah to fly to Earth and kill his ancestors, so he could not be born, grow up and eventually come to Saturn. The Earthling would be male with pink skin and yellow hair. He was not due here for

centuries, but he was coming. Cassini was
sure of it.

Since murder is against Saturnaa law -
just speaking of it gets citizens removed
from society – Cassini was imprisoned in the
dungeon. He had no family, so no one came
to visit him.

We offered Cassini clean clothes, but
he refused them, only wearing his ragtag,
green tunic. Cassini splashed water on
himself on occasion, but refused to shave, or
to comb or cut his matted hair. His appetite
was fair, but his spirits were low. When
asked how we could help him, he said
nothing could. Nothing, but to get rid of the
pink man's potential to come to Saturn.

We had no choice, but to keep him in
the dungeon for the rest of his natural life.
Cassini died at the age of 63 in his sleep one
night. He was buried in an unmarked
grave...

My head snapped up. Good Godlah!

The old man in the dirty, green tunics
had a name: Cassini.

The old man in the dirty, green tunics
had been right.

And I had seen a ghost.

My hands shook so violently that I dropped the volume. It landed on my foot, smarting. I picked it up with shaky hands, put it back, and scanned the bookshelves. There was an empty spot where the logs were that explained what to do if anyone from another world landed here.

July 6, 3005

My anger at the pink man from Earth had dissolved by the next day. Something in my heart told me that he was a good man. It was a battle between the little voice in my head, telling me the truth, and a bigger voice, telling it to shut up. This man held the fate of the Saturnaa people in his hands, but…

Why should he pay for the sins of his forefathers? I had heard stories about black people in America, committing crimes centuries ago, and whites punished and harassed other innocent blacks because of it. People who had nothing to do with the criminal's act. It wasn't right when they did it, and it wouldn't be right for us to do it.

Anyway, we met in the square, and
stood shoulder-to-shoulder. King Pulsar
stood on the jutting rock platform, looking
uneasy. His sister would know what to do, I
thought.

Questions from each district had been
collected, and the king answered them one-
by-one. When is the man from Earth
scheduled to leave? What is he doing here?
Does he have a third eye on his chest, a third
arm on his back, or a second private part?
King Pulsar, rolled his eyes, and tossed that
note aside. The crowd couldn't help but
chuckle. Pulsar collected himself, and
continued going through his stack of
questions. There were only two more. What
does this mean for us, the Saturnaa people?
What are we going to do with the pink
Earthling? King Pulsar seemed to look over
our heads, as he answered. "You know that
has to be decided by the populace in a vote.
Votes will be held next week, close to when
the Earthling is scheduled to leave." His
answer sounded rehearsed.

"I say we put him to death," Europa
shouted, a short, stout woman in a rust-
colored tunic I never liked. Her husband

grunted in agreement. "It's for the greater good of the Saturnaa."

King Pulsar held up a hand. "Murdering someone is against Saturnaa law. It's also against Godlah's commandments."

Europa grunted too, and pursed her mouth. She was done, but another man in the crowd, pulled on his whiskers, and sneered before giving his opinion. "Europa is right: those people are evil. They did heinous things to people on Earth and to the land there. They are the reason our ancestors left. If we let him go back to Earth, he will surely bring more people like him here to rape our people and our natural resources. We'll be back in chains again, just like our ancestors. Look at how prosperous we are. That couldn't be accomplished on Earth. We were downtrodden and poor there after slavery ended. And we were supposed to be freed? That didn't sound like freedom to me!" Others began to clap, nod, and mumble in agreement.

King Pulsar held up his hand again in protest, but it was in vain. I don't know why I did what I did, but probably would not do it again if I had the chance. I pushed through the crowd, and went to one of the king's guard. "Skoll!" Father Mimas shouted after me. "Brother, what are you doing?" Io bleated.

"Please," I whispered fiercely to the guard, "Ask the king to let me have the floor. I have been talking with the man from Earth."

He looked at me a while then recognition flickered in his eyes. He hastily jumped up to the mini stage to whisper in King Pulsar's ear. The king looked down at me with hesitation. He didn't want to turn over the floor to a seventeen-year-old boy, but what did he have to lose at this point? He was losing control of the crowd. The king gestured for me to come up to the stage.

Everyone was immediately quiet. I opened my mouth, but nothing came out at first. "Listen, everyone- "I stopped short, realizing that I was speaking English. I shook my head, as if to switch it back to the Saturnesh channel. "King Pulsar is right. Putting someone to death is not the Saturnaa way. Godlah states that He is the only one who can create life, and take it away. We have always been a Godlah-fearing people. Let's not stop being those kind of people now."

"All right then," Europa stated, "Let's not kill him. Let's just imprison him for the rest of his natural life in the dungeon, or send him to one of our moons." Once again, people grunted in agreement.

I cleared my throat, "I understand your position. I truly do. I love our settlement, and our people and don't want to put them at risk, but we can't simply imprison, or exile someone for life, who has committed no crime. And he would die on that moon. Jeff doesn't know how to permanently live anywhere, except Earth."

"Why not?" someone else stated, "Slaves were imprisoned for the rest of their natural lives, simply for the crime of having dark skin. Why should we use logic and mercy towards him and his kind when they didn't do it with us?"

"Because," I said, turning my crumby ring around and around on my finger, "It would be taking revenge on the wrong person. The Earthling has a wife of African descent and a baby daughter - "

"So he told you," Europa's husband piped up beside her, "He's scared. The Earthling will say anything to get you pity him, so we'll release him."

I looked the man in the eye, as I replied, "That very well may be true. But the Earthling Jeff is someone's son, as I am." I stopped, looking down at my hand, spinning the ring on my other hand, and looked up and scanned all those beige bodies in colorful tunics with diamonds on nearly every limb. "We," I said, as I caught my family's faces near the middle of the crowd, "are a strong people. We survived heinous hate crimes on Earth, but yet we are still in this world. If we can leave one planet for another, and build another successful civilization on it, surely, we can solve this problem. We will find a way around this that does not harm the Earthling. Right, King Pulsar?" I turned in his direction and bowed slightly.

"Y-yes," he stuttered. When I stood, I could see that beads of sweat had bloomed on the king's upper lip, even in the intense cold.

"This young man makes sense. My advisors and I will present some plans at our next meeting – in about two days - and the city will vote on them. Please, try not to worry. The Earthling is still in custody, and is being treated humanely."

Everyone looked at each other then slowly left the square. King Pulsar gave me a soft smile. I knew he was thanking me, but I had started to sweat too.

July 7, 3006

I came with a peace offering on my next visit with Earthling Jeff: a huge bowl of yamolite. He scarfed it down, like there was no tomorrow. As far as he knew, there was no tomorrow for him. I asked him if he needed anything after he finished.

Jeff ran his hand over his pink jaw, covered with dark, yellow stubble. "Can I have a shave?"

"I think we can arrange that," I said, scribbling it down on my paper. Then I finally got the nerve to ask him more about Earth.

"What do warm days feel like?"

"Kind of like being in a solar juice bath. Sunshine makes you feel good and happy."

"And birds? What do they sound like?"

Jeff pursed his lips and blew out air. A lilting, high-pitched melody escaped from them. "Kind of like that."

I stood entranced. It seemed forever before I found my tongue again. "What do grass and flowers feel like?"

"They are both soft, especially flower petals. Grass feels really good on bare feet."

"What is water rain like?"

"Little drops of water fall from the sky, cleaning everything, making everything grow, like the grass and flowers we just talked about. Rain smells nice, too; clean and fresh, like the Earth just had a bath."

I digested the information, my urge to smell, hear, and feel those things, stronger than ever. I suddenly felt stupid.

"Well," I mumbled, "I better go. You will get your shave. I promise."

Earthling Jeff was beyond words. I grabbed the empty yamolite bowl, and called for the guards to let me out.

July 8, 3006

I found a bible in the castle's log room that our ancestors left to us. I read some passages, and found one story in it particularly interesting. It just may be the answer to our problem. I will present it to King Pulsar and his advisors.

July 9, 3006

Today is the day. We will vote in the square on what to do with Earthling Jeff. First, the two options were presented. King Pulsar presented the solution I suggested, and another solution that he and his advisors created. We all went home to discuss which way each bio dome would vote, weigh the pros and cons of each solution.

We are to reconvene at the square before nightfall to cast our votes. Then they will be tallied.

July 10, 3006

We voted. This is my last entry. Hopefully, this isn't the last you will hear of the Saturnaa people, if this plan works.

Anyway, I pray to Godlah that everyone in His world, on every planet, has a long and happy life. In Godlah's name I pray. Amen.

Skoll

Epilogue

The boy wore his gold tunic again that day, as he entered Earthling Jeff's cell one last time. "We're sending you home," he said.

"Really? That's wonderful! Then why do you look so sad, Skoll? Is it because you will miss me?" he asked, his blue eyes narrowing in concern.

"That's some it. But it's also because," the boy said, turning his ring around and around on his finger, "you have to do something for us…"

"What?" Earthling Jeff asked.

"Don't worry. You will not be harmed. May I have a seat while I explain it to you?"

"Sure," Earthling Jeff said, scooting over on his sleeping mat to make room for the boy.

The guards escorted the pink astronaut from the dungeon, and out into the city with the teenaged boy, acting as tour guide. The citizens were still instructed to stay inside their homes, so the roads were empty. They showed the astronaut the square with Nat

Blackburn's statue, toured the row of shops and markets, learning dome, and Lake Calypso. The astronaut's blue eyes never stopped bucking in amazement.

They had saved the best and most important for last: a trip to Skoll's – the boy's - bio dome. He instructed the guards to wait outside while he and the pink astronaut went inside. After several minutes, the boy, his family, and the astronaut returned with a bulging sack and an infant on his hip, about 8 months old. "His foster parents let us have a few days with him. Please allow my sister to carry my nephew to your ship," the boy said before his face crumbled. The rest of his family looked on with leaking eyes. The pink man nodded, taking the sack from the boy. The boy kissed the baby's plump cheek, and handed him to the teenaged girl. The family and guards began walking towards the spaceship.

"I nearly forgot," the boy said, sniffling, when they got to the ship." He undid the rope of diamonds around his neck and took the ring off his finger. "Put these in the bag, too." The astronaut complied, and offered his hand. Neither the guards, nor the family knew what that meant.

"It's Earth custom to greet or leave on a friendly note."

The Saturnaa people extended their hands, too. He chuckled. "Now you each grasp my hand, and shake it." They all took clumsy turns, shaking the astronaut's hand.

"Thank you for your kindness," the pink man said, his blue eyes tearing above his oxygen mask, scanning their faces and everything around them. "What a beautiful place," he muttered, tilting his head up towards Saturn's arcing, iridescent rings. He then opened the hatch to his spaceship, and reached for the infant. Weeping, the girl handed him over then folded into her family in a group hug.

Once the pink man was settled in his rocket with the hatch firmly closed, he took off the oxygen mask. He settled the baby down comfortably, and put the sack nearby. He immediately hopped on the radio. "Mission control? Mission control? This is Jeff McNeely. I am on my way back to Earth, but I won't be returning alone…"

*****

There had been two agendas in the log books if someone landed on Saturn. Many voted for the latter.

The first was to evacuate everyone to one of Saturn's moons, but it would take too long to get everyone there before another visitor landed on Saturn. Nat Blackburn didn't have nearly as many people to transport when he left Earth. Besides, that was their home. It's one place you don't turn and run from anyone – at least not anymore, they reasoned. Their ancestors had pretty much been pushed from their home planet. They were not going to allow history to repeat itself.

They were "staying." The people busied themselves burning every last personal possession that they owned. Workers demolished the castle, buildings, the Godlah temple, and bio domes. Even the beautiful statue of Ignatius Blackburn VI was broken up into so many pieces that it simply looked like boulders. And that was the intent; leave no trace of human evidence on Saturn.

After all of the Saturnaa people's material things and dwellings were gone, they all marched, naked, to the huge lake, Calypso. They had stripped and burned their clothing, too, because they didn't want any clothing to float up to the water's surface, or wash ashore. All diamond jewelry and décor was buried deep in a pit of Saturn's freezing soil.

King Pulsar gave one last speech, and said a prayer. Godlah will understand, he said. We can't possibly let them come and hurt us again. Don't be afraid.

One-by-one, they waded in. A crumby's sting is poisonous, and there were many in the lake.

Days before this, the boy everyone knew as Skoll had learned about baby Moses from The Bible in the castle's log room. He presented this concept to King Pulsar, and nearly everyone agreed. His nephew, now hurtling through the stars to Earth, would be the Baby Moses in the bulrushes, to carry on the proud, resourceful, Saturnaa spirit, its rich history. Baby Janus was the only child young enough on the planet to not remember his life on Saturn, yet he was barely off Io's breast. There were either expectant mothers at this time, or other children who were already toddlers.

"Make us proud, Janus," the boy whispered, just as a crumby stung his ankle with its needle-like proboscis. He felt himself go weak, and slip under the water with the others to ironically become food for the crustaceans they had dined on for centuries.

Astronaut Jeff McNeely and the baby, now a year old, were held in quarantine upon their return to Earth. NASA staff communicated with Jeff through intercom while they were isolated. He was questioned incessantly about this alleged human colony on Saturn, the child, and the items they allegedly gave him.

It was incredible, but Jeff wasn't sent with a woman who he could have possibly gotten pregnant on the voyage. The child was about twelve months old when Jeff had returned, less than a year later. The math and the lack of female company on the rocket supported Jeff's statement.

It was incredible, but where could the astronaut have possibly gotten the bag, and all the strange items in it?

"I know. I know," Jeff answered, "I wouldn't have believed it myself if I hadn't seen it. It's true though. They are the Saturnaa; the descendants of Africans and other blacks who left here centuries ago."

There was a pause. "That did happen here in 1900, but your camera didn't show people there."

"They controlled what I recorded."

There was a pause.

"All right," the voice crackled through the intercom, "get some rest, and we'll talk more about this later."

Jeff McNeely was relieved of his astronaut duty, shortly after. NASA swore him to secrecy – in writing - about what he had seen on Saturn. On one condition, Jeff said: you allow me and my wife to adopt Janus. He is NOT an alien, and will not be treated as such. Fair enough, NASA said.

They immediately planned a new mission to Saturn. We finally found intelligent life on another planet! But the satellite revealed the same thing that Jeff's camera had: nothing but ice and rocks and a large lake. They sent two more to capture pictures, just to be sure. After all, Saturn is a huge planet.

Still no diamond-bedecked people in colorful tunics.

No proud statue in a city square.

No marketplace.

No bio domes.

NASA was left, frowning and scratching their heads.

Former astronaut, Jeff, and his wife raised Janus (soon renamed Jay), alongside their daughter, Aurora. They told everyone that the boy had been adopted. Close in age, the children got along well – for the most part. They were both excellent students who could be seen in each others' rooms studying together then teasing each other the next moment. Aurora was boy-crazy, and Jay was the old soul; the responsible one.

Time rolled on. Jeff and his wife, Zinnia, sprouted a few gray hairs on their heads and a few lines in their faces. Aurora had just turned sixteen in March, and Jay was about to in November. The boy was an excellent writer who was a star in the high school newspaper, and had an almost obsessive interest in science, especially astronomy. He looked just like "his people," too, with a beige complexion and clover honey eyes. Jay kept his curls long, like them too, to the nape of his neck.

On the evening of Jay's sixteenth birthday, Jeff knocked on Jay's bedroom door. "Come in," the boy said, weakly. He was exhausted from the dizzying day of bowling, a huge birthday cake, presents, etc., and was already in bed.

His father entered his room with a somber expression and a bag, made with material that he had never seen. He closed the door, and turned Jay's desk chair around, facing him before he sat.

"What's wrong, dad?"

"Nothing. I just have to tell you something important. *Show* you something important. I made a promise to do this when you turned sixteen."

Jay sat up in bed. Jeff set the bag down on the floor, and slowly began to pull things from it. "Your real name is Janus, son. You were born on Saturn…"

Janus/Jay's sat in bed, staring at nothing in his room in particular, head spinning. Then he picked up each item, and studied them closely:

A rope of diamonds, the size of peanuts. Familiarity stabbed his gut, as he got a flashback of his own chubby infant hand, grabbing at this necklace on someone…someone…

A beautiful ring, shaped like an animal he had never seen before, with diamond eyes.

Two round and polished crustacean shells that had been fashioned into what looked like currency.

A small bag of rocks with different facial expressions, etched into them.

And three thick volumes. One said "English," on the cover, and the others had a language on it that he didn't know.

Janus/Jay put the ring on his left ring finger, and it fit perfectly, as if it had been made for him. Then with shaking hands, he picked up the volume that said "English," and opened it. A note had been tucked inside:

Dear Nephew Janus,

I know this is a lot to take in now, but you must know who you are. Read this to find out. I pass the torch on to you, dearest nephew, to keep our story going. We love you so much.

Uncle Skoll and family

Janus/Jay slowly turned the page, and began reading.

March 15, 3005

I am Skoll, named for one of my planet's minor moons…

Other books by Sean C. Wright, available on Amazon

Feel free to learn more about her at
www.seanarchy.wordpress.com.

The Adventures of Bootsy the Boston (2019)
3 tales about a sweet, energetic doggie who lives life to the fullest with boy and girl human.

The Adventures of Bootsy the Boston

Written by Sean C. Wright   Illustrated by Jason Neeley

Glo Ro Saves Best Treasure Chest (2018)
Tainted by family tragedy, 16-year-old amateur gumshoe, Glorious Day Roberts knows she must give her all to save her favorite store.

Mary & Jerry Canary & Hot Doggie (2018)
Young twin canaries learn life lessons while teaching them to your children as well. A series.

A Gathering of Butterflies (2015)
A quartet of short stories about strong, yet vulnerable
women of color.

Honey Riley (2014)
A flame-haired clairvoyant can't predict her own painful fate.

Made in the USA
Columbia, SC
06 October 2020